ALSO BY SAM LIPSYTE

the
FUN
PARTS

the FUN PARTS

SAM LIPSYTE

FARRAR, STRAUS AND GIROUX NEW YORK

Farrar, Straus and Giroux
18 West 18th Street, New York 10011

Copyright © 2013 by Sam Lipsyte
All rights reserved
Printed in the United States of America
First edition, 2013

These stories previously appeared, in slightly different form, in the following publications: *J&L Illustrated* ("Ode to Oldcorn"), *Jane* ("Snacks"), *McSweeney's* ("Peasley"), *The New Yorker* ("The Climber Room," "The Dungeon Master," "Deniers," "The Republic of Empathy"), *Open City* ("Nate's Pain Is Now"), *The Paris Review* ("The Worm in Philly," "This Appointment Occurs in the Past"), *Playboy* ("The Real-Ass Jumbo" as "The Gunderson Prophecy," "The Wisdom of the Doulas"), and *Tin House* ("Expressive").

Library of Congress Cataloging-in-Publication Data
Lipsyte, Sam, 1968–
    The fun parts / Sam Lipsyte. — 1st ed.
        p.   cm.
    Short stories.
    ISBN 978-0-374-29890-6 (hardcover : alk. paper)
    I. Title.

PS3562.I648F86 2013
813'.54—dc23   2012029534

Designed by Jonathan D. Lippincott

www.fsgbooks.com
www.twitter.com/fsgbooks • www.facebook.com/fsgbooks

1   3   5   7   9   10   8   6   4   2

FOR SUSANNAH

CONTENTS

the
CLIMBER
ROOM

The sign in the Sweet Apple kitchen declared it a nut-free zone, and every September somebody, almost always a dad, cracked the usual stupid joke. The gag, Laura, the school director, told Tovah, would either mock the school's concern for potentially lethal legumes or else suggest that despite the sign's assurance, not everyone at Sweet Apple could boast of sanity.

Today, as Tovah leaned into the fridge to adjust the lunch bag heap, a skinny gray-haired man in a polo shirt, old enough to be the grandfather of the girl who called him "Papa" as he nudged her toward the cubbies, winked at Tovah, pointed to the sign.

Here it came, the annual benediction.

"Nut free!" Papa said. "Oh, no! Guess I'd better scram!"

He looked at Tovah as though expecting some response, but what? Tolerant smile? Snappy retort? Hand job? These older fathers with their second, "doing-it-right-this-time" families were the worst. This version stuck out a large, knuckly hand that seemed locked in a contest for supremacy with his heavy platinum watch.

"Randy Goat," the man said.

Tovah figured she had misheard.

"Tovah Gold," she said, and shook his hand, or, rather, a few of his supple fingers.

"And this is Dezzy."

"Dezzy!" Tovah said, recognized the girl now. She sank to a knee, which was not only the proper way to address children

3

but a nifty evasive maneuver vis-à-vis their crypto-creepy pro-genitors. "Hi, Dezzy. Do you remember me? I tagged along with Laura on the home visit a few weeks ago. You showed me your new sparkly shoes."

"Sparkle shoes," said Dezzy.

"Sparkle, of course."

"Right," Randy said. "I was out of town when you guys popped by."

The place had been enormous, dizzying, a living (well, not quite living) embodiment (not embodiment, precisely) of the aspirational sconce porn that Tovah sometimes indulged in online or at magazine racks.

"We met your wife," Tovah said. "She was so nice."

Tovah still blanked on the family name. She was stuck with Goat.

"I remember with my older children," the man said. "You guys like to do a little recon. Find out if we keep our kids in filth while we boost skag all day. But I guess we passed. We good, God-fearin' folks, I swears."

Tovah stared at him, unsure of Laura's preferred reply to such a performance. She was new to the pre-K world, and just part-time, temporary. Tovah had been an administrative coordinator at an East Side prep school for years, until the school brought back the retired headmaster to replace her. The crash had made crumb snatchers of the toniest. The headmaster had run the school. Now he ran the office, and Tovah, at home, ran a lot of hot water for non-revitalizing soaks. The offer from Sweet Apple, managed through a distant family friend, had saved her.

"Sorry to shock you," Randy Goat said now. "Just fun-nin'."

"You didn't shock me," said Tovah, though the word "skag," the old-timey TV creak of it, intrigued her.

"A tightass," Randy Goat said. "Good. It means you'll be careful with my kid."

Now other children tore past, monogrammed backpacks jouncing. Laura jogged up in an outfit she'd recently described as "business yoga casual."

"Mr. Gautier," she said. "Wonderful."

"You know to call me Randy, Laura. You look radiant. You must have bloomed with love this summer."

Laura blushed. "Not quite."

"Just a fling? Sounds fun."

Tovah pictured another universe where, without hesitation, she could slap Randy Gautier's smug, maybe once sensual old-man mouth. Laura was annoying, but she didn't deserve this spinster baiting, especially from a geezer. Tovah wasn't that far from cat ladyhood herself, though she believed—had staked her life on the belief—that everything always changed at the last minute. The right man, or even woman (what did it matter, really?), would just appear and, for goddamn certain, the right baby. Which meant any baby, within reason. Race or gender didn't matter, but spine on the inside would be nice. Now an unknown force, perhaps the man's shimmering wrist piece, whipped her back through conjectured space-time, far from the cool, lavender room where she cradled her perfect newborn. She stood with her hand on Desdemona Gautier's silky skull while the girl's father bent down to address her.

"It's going to be a great day, sweetie. The first of many great days. Just do whatever Laura and Tovah tell you."

The Goat Man winked at Tovah again.

Tovah treated him to the smile she once bestowed upon the creative writing professor who told her that some people were meant to write poetry and others, like Tovah, to treasure it.

She'd proved that incontinent toad wrong, for a few years, anyway.

Tovah's D'Agostino's card wouldn't beep her the rebate. She feigned a pressing appointment, offered to pay full price for her crackers and sodium-free vegetable broth. The woman at the register looked at Tovah as though she'd chucked a diamond brooch into the Hudson.

"I can just swipe for you," she said, slid an extra card from beneath the cash drawer.

"Save it for somebody worthy," Tovah said.

"Hey," the woman said. "We need the wood."

"What's that?"

"You didn't die for my sins, lady. So don't go building a cross for yourself. We need the wood."

Tovah gave a feral grin. By midnight tonight, fueled by soup and crackers, she would have her first verse in years.

"Thank you," Tovah said. "You don't even know."

"I know you need crazy bitch pills," the woman muttered, but Tovah, lost in private, triumphal noise, did not catch it.

By midnight Tovah lay on the couch with a stomachache. A miniature swordsman flensed her gut with his foil, or so went an intriguing image that had come to her as she puked up the crackers, the soup, and the Chinese entrées she'd ordered after the crackers ran out. She never ate like this. She kept her slim figure with a subsistence diet of iced espressos, store-cut cheese cubes, and a few dry salads a day. But she remembered that back when she really wrote poetry, she ate a lot of greasy food, with no gastric regret. The extra weight had just made her voluptuous. She'd been so young.

Now she was thirty-six and in one eating spree had become a vile sack of fat and rot. In her vision of herself she was not even obese, but more like a bloated carcass gaffed from a lake. There on the couch, her belly flopped over her jeans, the new chin she'd acquired in about five hours damp and rashy, rank scents curled from her pores and, especially, from her crotch, whenever she tugged at her waistband to ease the ache. It was all so awful, evil, so unlike the Tovah of recent years, of modified appetites and reduced expectations, that her corpse-body surged with something revoltingly, smearishly pleasing. She felt slimy, garbage-juice sexy. Her hand jerked inside her underwear for relief. She pictured the actual gaffer leaning over the gunwale: rugged, with kind, lustful eyes under a brocaded cap. Sparkle eyes. Tovah's legal pad, upon which she'd written only the title of her poem, "Needing the Wood," slid to the carpet. Her fountain pen, caught against an embroidered yellow pillow, impaled it.

Morning light woke her, but Tovah's half-closed eyes bent the rays back into a dream about a sun-stabbed land of which Tovah was philosopher-queen. She could retain her crown only by mastering a vintage pinball machine set atop an onyx plinth. The flippers stuck, and the holes were the mouths of female poets. A silver ball plopped into the maw of Dickinson. A voice in the head of her dreamself told Tovah not to "skin lip."

She woke again, rose from the couch, saw the stained cartons of kung pao chicken, sesame chicken, sweet and sour chicken, and mystery moo shoo. She retched. She took a shower and made gunpowder tea and sat on the toilet and sighed. She had a date tonight.

It would be odd to see Sean again. Her best friend in college, Callie, had a brother, and everyone had agreed that this lean black-haired wonder was bound for an extraordinary life. Sean might direct a morally resonant movie, or design a marvelous bridge, or climb a heretofore unscalable mountain both to prove his prowess and deliver medicine to a snowed-in camp on the far slope. He had a keen mind, a daredevil physicality, a conscience. You could picture him leading large, semi-whimsical social movements.

At his sister's party during one Christmas break years before, Sean's graciousness, even more than his charisma, had undone Tovah. Sean made the rounds, checked on everybody's drinks, lavished his attentions on the shy. When he walked up and handed Tovah a daiquiri and they spoke for a few moments about turtles, or tortoises of great size and longevity, Tovah felt something magical and formfitting slip over her: a tunic of light. This was the way Jesus must have worked, some petty wonder talk while revelation sunk its celestial needle. An artificial insemination of the soul. Soon Sean drifted away, perhaps to knock up other guests.

Tovah never saw him again and thought about him constantly. She waited for word of his victories. Callie nourished her with stories about new jobs and cities, so that Sean became a character in some corny but secretly enthralling serial adventure. He worked on oil rigs in the Gulf of Mexico, wrote experimental screenplays in Gobi desert yurts, enrolled in architecture school, film school, medical school (but only for research, with no intention of doctoring). He had undertaken a scientifically significant balloon journey. But after a while the stories got hazy. Callie said something about a junk habit.

Tovah wondered if Sean was the type who peaked just before setting off into the world, the boy the gang bets on before they understand life. A sad notion, but she still wanted to see him. He'd reached out to her through several friends (not Callie, though, who'd broken with Tovah over a misunderstanding about the location of a brunch spot). Sean's contact was not random, but certainly sudden.

His interest surprised her. People had eased away from Tovah. She had become a tad too prickly, or self-sufficient. Maybe her empathy seemed strained. Unfair, this last, as she really felt for others, and with them, but it never quite came across. That's what creative writing was for. She knew better, from so many workshops, than to suggest that poetry existed to express one's feelings, though infuriatingly, hers did.

A baby, however, especially a baby bred to be lean and coal haired and jade eyed and slant smiled, like Sean, could learn to express Tovah's feelings, too, without the torture of words.

Out on Broadway, Tovah stepped into a hat boutique, the kind of sparse, dusty affair you assume would be a depression's first prey, but here it stood. Tovah hated hats, or could never conceive of a hat that would suit her, except maybe a floppy straw thing she could wear to the beach with sunglasses and coquettishly unflattering sandals. She'd lug along books in a canvas bag, but when would she get to the beach? She lived on an island, sure, but that didn't mean she numbered among those permitted to go to the beach.

"Can I help you?" said the salesgirl.

She seemed, but didn't look, fifteen.

"Who comes in here?" Tovah asked.

"People looking for hats."

"That is twisted."

Tovah felt funny. Maybe she hadn't really bounced back from last night's death feast.

Maybe what she'd been on the couch was pregnant, though only ignorance could make it true. You could reckon the dates, track the cycles, but then certain facts press down. You couldn't be pregnant if you hadn't been laid in three years. A devout Catholic could still hope, but not Tovah. She'd never even considered herself the maternal type. She didn't believe there was such a temperament, unless one assembled it in the culture factory along with images of women as radiant white creatures traipsing through summer fields with their tanned, though still white, spawn.

Those were the old lies. The newer ones claimed that all committed mothers could also manage begemmed careers, that only the weak or untalented had to choose. But even the mothers at Sweet Apple, not to mention her former school, could not disguise their struggle. Instead they sought catharsis in their comic monologues about the slog, or the sick joke of being marked as both mediocre mothers and lousy colleagues.

Some mothers at Sweet Apple had gleaned an even greater shift: the shame in procreation. People glared at families, at mothers. Nobody got up for pregnant women on the subway anymore. The planet couldn't sustain more mouths. So stand, greedy lady.

Tovah had picked her side years before. No peace-shredding hominid would find shelter in her womb. She loved to play with the pre-K kids, but live with one? Then something embarrassing and maybe purely chemical occurred. She wanted a baby. That was all. She still believed everything she believed, cultivated privacy and solitude, and, despite her attachment to the Sweet Apple tykes, believed childlessness the noble course (yes, your kid might cure cancer, but probably he'd grow up to play video games or, if the world followed its current path, huddle in a gulch slurping gulchwater and recalling the magnificence of video games). But she wanted a baby. That's what her body was for, in the cruel scheme of things, and she craved the bleakness of biology. It didn't matter if the baby was hers, except it absolutely did. She wanted to carry it and give birth to it and breast-feed it and live in a natural cocoon with it for as long as possible, with somebody on the outside slipping everything she needed through a slim vent. In this way life would be joyful instead of nearly unlivable. The part of her that she'd always trusted knew this was crazy, but that part had also, one had to admit, led her to this grim limbo.

Tovah started across the street for a cleansing smoothie. Somebody shouted her name. Mr. Gautier strode toward her. He had a sharp-boned swagger and wore a hat, a baseball cap, stitched with the words GLYPH SYSTEMS.

"Mr. Gautier," she called.

"Randy."

"Hello," Tovah said.

Mr. Gautier put a hand on Tovah's shoulder, took a few hard breaths. He dipped his head and spat something pebble sized onto the pavement. Tovah noticed the tiny hearing aid that lurked behind a shrub of ear hair.

"You played hooky today," he said.

"It was a day off. I'm only part-time."

"Did you hear what happened over there?"

She could picture only worst-case scenarios. Fires, floods, a collapsed ceiling in the lunch nook, a child pincered in that window sash the caretaker still hadn't fixed. Or maybe Laura had finally snapped, kicked one of what she liked to call the Future Date Rapists of America in the skull. Boys, Laura had told her, were bad for schools, bad for society.

Which wasn't to say, Laura added, that she didn't love the cuties to death.

"Dezzy was in the climber room," Mr. Gautier said, "and she fell off the . . . whatever it is."

"The climber."

"The climber," Mr. Gautier said. "They could just say jungle gym. What's the big diff?"

"Is Dezzy okay?" Tovah asked. "Those pads on the floor are pretty soft."

"She's fine. That's not the point. She freaked out, and she cried for you. I'm convinced she feels more comfortable and confident with you around."

"That's sweet. She's so delicious. Really."

Tovah had heard other teachers use "delicious" this way. It seemed natural, but also strange, which maybe described cannibalism in general.

"A delight," she amended.

"Of course she's a delight," Mr. Gautier said. "She's my daughter. So anyway, I worked it out with Laura. You'll be changing your days so you can be there every morning Dezzy is."

"You what?" Tovah said.

"Don't worry, you don't have to do a thing. I took care of it."

"Look, I'm flattered, but I picked my days already. I think Dezzy is great, but so are the other kids, and I'm all set in my schedule."

"Do a search," Mr. Gautier said.

A low snarl threaded his voice. There was something bird-like about his face, she noticed now, specifically a big scavenger bird, maybe a turkey vulture. But a handsome turkey vulture. It was confusing.

"Excuse me?"

"When you get home, open your browser and do a search on me."

"Okay."

She couldn't believe she'd agreed. What a bastard.

"Then you can do a search on me," Tovah said.

She hoped her snideness bore no hint of tease. She hoped she sounded young enough to make him feel old.

"I did," Mr. Gautier said. "When they aren't mired in post-modern feminist crap, your poems are really good. Couldn't find anything recent online. What happened?"

"Life," Tovah said, startled.

"I'm thinking maybe the opposite. Look, we should be friends. I like the effect you have on Dezzy."

"It's been two days," Tovah said.

"Those first few are the ones that count. Anyway, thanks for rejiggering your schedule. It means a lot, and you shall be rewarded."

"Rewarded? I'm a professional."

"No, you're not," Mr. Gautier said. "That's why you're good."

She figured she'd have to be patient, but the Goat popped right up on her computer search and dominated the many pages of results that followed. Math prodigy Randolph Gautier had dropped out of a North Jersey high school in 1973 and hitched out to Palo Alto. He would have seized a silicon throne but for some purloined software here, a botched algorithm there. Still, he'd done just fine. He'd sold his company, Glyph Systems, for tens of millions, though in interviews he seemed bitter about it. He told *RadTech* magazine that Bill Gates had an IQ of seventy-four.

The man had made money in computers. Was this fact the object of her search? There were plenty of rich oldies in the neighborhood. Then she noticed another branch of search hits, sites that mentioned Gautier in relation to artistic foundations, to his funding of a poetry journal called *Glyphonym*. She'd never heard of the journal or any of the poets listed in the index, but the bound editions looked swank. Photos of a launch party in a grand ballroom featured charitable omnipotent people chuckling over cocktails. No real poet would want a poem in that journal, but the party looked like vulgar fun, or at least better than a night on the couch locked in a frigonometric fugue state, sour sweet-and-sour sweat soaked through the cushions, although Tovah did, to her surprise, look back on that evening with fondness. "Needing the Wood" had a few lines now, borrowed, perhaps, and in Sanskrit, but indelibly on the page.

The shock about Sean was his shock of white hair. It looked regal but incongruous with the dark-locked boy she'd known. He stood and seemed to bow as she approached the table, a fairly formal gesture for a place that specialized in artisanal scrapple.

"Sean!" she called with cheerful volume, as though to cover for her disappointment in his follicles.

"Tovah!" Sean said. "Awesome!"

They hugged, and Tovah's chin grazed his collarbone. That zap, the hot, sweet charge of the party long ago, tingled. She wanted Sean to save her and screw her and give her a baby. After that, maybe he'd have to leave.

"You look great," Tovah said.

"If that's true, I owe it to the mighty sport of handball. I play with the Spanish gentlemen at the playground. It's an epic workout. You look really good, too. Seriously."

"I never exercise and I rarely eat. It's a winning plan."

"I think you're meant to be a little heavier, though. You're tall and skinny with big, beautiful bones."

"Big bones?"

"Totes. I know it's a euphemism for chubby girls, but you just happen to be hot with slightly extra-large bones. I always wanted to jump them. That night we talked. That was an epic night."

They hadn't even heard the specials and he'd already mentioned their magic moment.

"Man," he said. "What's it been? Twenty years?"

"Sixteen."

"Oh, that's better."

"How's your sister?" Tovah asked. "I haven't spoken with her in a long time."

"She's good. I mean evil. She works for this huge rape-a-licious law firm."

"Is she still married?"

"Totes."

"What's 'totes'?"

"Sorry, I work with a lot of young people. I pick up their lingo. Anyway, man, Tovah, you do look really good."

Was it possible he could be a moron and still be her savior?

"Where do you work?"

"Right now I'm involved with a new start-up," Sean said. "It's hard to explain. We make apps for apps, basically."

"So that pays well?"

"No, not yet. Meantime I'm working with organic food materials. Mostly flour items."

"Like a muffin shop?"

"Yeah, pretty much."

"I'm a part-time preschool teacher right now."

"Sounds epic," Sean said. "Little kids."

"I love kids," said Tovah. "But the politics . . ."

Or could she be the moron?

A young waiter arrived without menus and explained the ordering process, which involved a few crucial decisions about sides and beverages but a surrender of volition in the realm of entrées. Tonight was Thursday, which meant Pennsylvania-style scrapple.

"What exactly is scrapple?" Tovah asked.

"It's Mennonite soul food," Sean said.

The waiter rolled his eyes.

"It's everything from the pig except the meat," he said. "Organs, hooves, eyelashes, lips. It's all pressed together in a loaf. I, personally, love it."

"Sounds kind of tref," Tovah said.

"*Très* tref, dollface," the waiter said. "After dinner you can join a settlement and redeem yourself."

"Whoa there, buddy," Sean said.

"It's okay. I'm a Yid," the waiter said.

"Really?" Tovah said.

"Totes," the waiter said.

"Look, I think I'm going to leave," Tovah said. "I actually prefer pig eyelashes as a separate dish."

"Of course," Sean said. "Let's go."

They walked the streets for a while, laughed at the shitty waiter and the perspectival complexity of time. It reminded Tovah of those play scenes from eighth grade. Lovers by the creek or at the carnival. Something about the moon. Now they leaned on a playground fence. Beyond it, in the last of the light, children stalked each other with neon water rifles.

Sean looked at Tovah, pinched the collar of her shirt.

"Twenty years later, and I still feel attracted to you."

"Sixteen years," Tovah said. "I had no idea you liked me. I was so smitten. You were the genius. You were going to do all the wonderful things."

"Yeah, well."

"What happened?"

"Nothing happened," Sean said. "I've had all sorts of adventures. Good times, bad times. You know I've had my share . . ."

"Seriously," Tovah said.

She must have clawed out of the womb saying that.

"Seriously, I wasn't measuring myself against a prophecy of me."

"We were," Tovah said.

"Well, then, fuck you, Big Bones. That's your problem. And what are you doing that's so great? Anybody can play with kids."

"I'm also a poet."

"And you have a blog, I'm guessing?"

"I'm sorry," Tovah said. "You're right. I'm being abrasive. I get scared of intimacy. I flail."

"That's so cool."

"Let's start again. No more scrapple."

"I don't think so," Sean said. "Whatever the opposite of compatible is, that's us."

"Incompatible?" Tovah said.

"If you say so, wordsmith. Thing is, we both need the same crap. Somebody with money, and security, and also did I mention money? To shore up our egos. To nurture our unrealistic dreams."

"Yes," Tovah said. "That's actually true. That's an insight."

"Thank you," Sean said. "I used to be very promising."

"Can I ask you something?"

"Are you going to ask whether my hair turned white slowly or overnight?"

"Do you want me to?" Tovah said.

"Well, let me tell you a story. I was working on a guide boat out of the Solomon Islands."

Sean spoke into the darkness for a while, telling a mesmerizing, no doubt spurious tale. Tovah realized that she didn't care about him or his saga or the whiteness of his hair one whit. She could never mate with a man who called her Big Bones, even once, even in jest. She could never expose her eggs to such a jerk.

The climber room admitted six kids and one teacher at a time. The other children had to wait in the next room at their sand tables and clay stations. Tovah stood near the varnished wooden bars and watched Dezzy scale the ladder. This day had once been her day off.

Laura had called her soon after she'd talked to Mr. Gautier.

"Is this standard at Sweet Apple?" Tovah had asked. "Letting a parent dictate schedules?"

"He's not dictating. He made a request."

"What's the diff?"

"Tovah, I understand how this might seem concerning to you. But you're just here temporarily. Mr. Gautier has been part of the school family for many years. His yearly donation keeps us afloat. I don't want to disappoint him. That would be concerning to me. I don't want to say that if you don't abide by his request, there's a chance you might not be able to continue with us."

"You don't want to say what?"

"I believe you heard me."

"What if I just quit?"

"God, can you afford that? Lucky you. Can I quit with you? Do you have us covered?"

"Okay, Laura. I understand. It's okay."

"You're a real sweetheart," Laura said.

"I'm a schmuck," Tovah said.

"Always a fine line."

Tovah winced admiringly.

Now Dezzy turned from the ladder and shoved herself at Tovah's shoulder. Her frizzy hair scratched Tovah's cheek. The girl's breath carried sour fruit.

"I love you, Tovah!" Dezzy said, gurgled through surplus

saliva. Desdemona wasn't slow, just charmless, a sloppy need machine.

One of the other kids, a funny boy named Ewen, tugged on Tovah's jeans.

"Tovah," he said. "Can we read about the tigers again?"

Because Laura did in fact care about the boys and didn't want them to notice her revulsion, they'd become Tovah's responsibility.

"You can change them, the boys," Laura had told her. "Erase the predator patterns in their brains. Make them docile and generous. I'd do it myself, but I get so nauseated."

Tovah's Dezzy duty was a drag. She wanted to read to Ewen, but if Dezzy didn't want to join them, the morning would turn dire. Dezzy would collapse and wail. A real Trojan widow scene. It made Tovah wonder what went on at the House of Gautier. Randy Goat hadn't been making drop-offs or pickups this week. A young Tibetan woman came instead. And what did Mrs. Gautier do with her time? Or was that blond woman at the home visit even Dezzy's mother? Now Tovah found the narrative becoming dense. Dense wouldn't do. She was ready to wrap this up, find another—what did they call it?—situation.

Dezzy licked and nibbled Tovah's neck. Tovah hoisted the girl away from her.

"You don't want to skin lip?" Dezzy said.

"What? What did you say?"

"Ouchie. Put me down."

"Tigers, Tovah," Ewen said, tugged.

Mr. Gautier offered too much money for the babysitting job. It was more like a call girl's fee, even factoring in Dezzy's unpleasantness, but this was no era to demur. Tovah took the gig. It would be a noon-to-midnight shift on Saturday. Mr. Gautier had meetings, a benefit dinner.

Tovah had never babysat, not even in high school, but at least she was starting at the top. This wasn't a few hours at the neighbor's house, with Tovah paid in cable TV and leftover casserole. This was big bucks to encamp in a palace on Central Park West and monitor a brat while Mr. and Mrs. Gautier lorded it over the city's top-shelf kowtowers. Maybe they'd bring her white-frosted cake in swanned-up tinfoil. Everything seemed so pathetic and exciting.

She knew she should mention the offer to Laura, but she enjoyed the secret, side-business feel of it. There was something odd about Mr. Gautier, to be sure, but even if he returned home in his tux, tipsy from champagne, and his wife excused herself and retired to what she might refer to as her chambers, and when she was gone Mr. Gautier, while plucking sharp green bills from his silver clip, accidentally brushed his well-preserved knuckles against her breast or her bosom or her (perhaps let's just say specifically) unusually responsive (based on informal polls of friends) nipple, and they locked eyes and giggled and then, for no reason at all, kissed, skin lipped, as some tiny persons would have it, until they heard a noise, a door off the den or a loose board in the refurbished hallway, maybe the wife returning to the kitchen for her bedtime book, one of those wretched memoirs with a blurred photo of a schoolgirl on the jacket, and upon hearing the noise, they, Randy and Tovah, froze and broke apart in thrilled fright—even if all of that happened, she wasn't sure she would tell Laura. In fact, she knew she wouldn't tell her, so why mention the babysitting job at all?

Besides, it would be awkward in a few years, when Tovah was—and let's be totally random here—Randy's new wife, the mother of his baby, and Tovah found herself, for example, president of the board of Sweet Apple, which had the power to hire and fire directors as she (or she and the board) saw fit. Of course, without question, Tovah would endorse a renewal of Laura's contract. The woman needed a viable wardrobe, but she'd proved herself a more than capable employee. Besides, there would be so many other things to worry about, such as the transformation of *Glyphonym* from a ludicrous glossy bursting with trust fund doggerel to a rigorous journal where the best poets, regardless of tradition, would connect with one another and a larger audience. A few poems a year by Tovah would not be unseemly. Other editors did it.

Plenty more so-called luxury problems might rear their plush heads. You had to hire the right people, make certain that the nanny wasn't teaching the baby Cantonese by mistake, or the cook wasn't drizzling the wrong oils on Tovah's salads, not to mention the guaranteed Stukka dives of bitchery from the ditched blond wife. Tovah didn't know a thing about her, but the woman's gold-digging implements had been edged enough to carve out some precious metal from the Randolph Gautier vein. Doubtless they could leave nasty divots in the flesh of her usurper. Still, the state of alert would be worth it because of the baby, the baby that would be hers and also nestled in cozy plenitude, the combination she never thought possible.

Dezzy didn't come to school on Friday, so Tovah e-mailed Mr. Gautier to make sure the date, or the job, rather, was still on. He did not respond all day.

Sweet Apple exhausted her. Her boys—Ewen, Juanito, Medgar, and Shalom—had been hanging all over her, begging her read to them or play airplane or lie on the carpet as a launchpad. Tovah wasn't sure if she had deactivated their predator wiring. It was hard to tell when they were such relentless puppies. She fell asleep on the train home and nearly missed her stop. She'd need some quality rest to handle Dezzy tomorrow, if that was still her destiny.

The call finally came as she finished her radicchio.

"You e-mail me?"

"Yes. About tomorrow."

"It's better to just call me. I don't check e-mail much. But I see your e-mail in my browser. It scared me. I didn't open it. Does it say you're not coming? Don't tell me you're not coming. Jesus fucking Christ. I counted on you. I put my neck on the chopping block convincing Connie that you weren't just some tight little piece of . . . well, whatever, but a real—"

"I'm coming, Randy Goat!" Tovah cried.

"Huh?"

"I mean, I just e-mailed to confirm. I'm certainly planning on coming to watch Dezzy, so you and your wife shouldn't worry about a—"

"My wife?"

"Yes, I met her at the home visit."

"Connie's my sister. That's who you saw. She's always trying to horn in on the raising of Dezzy. I guess I let her. It's easier that way. Dezzy's adopted. She was my goddaughter, and her parents were killed. Okay, what the hell are we doing? Are we phone buddies or something?"

"No," Tovah said.

"You bet your ass we aren't. I'll see you tomorrow at eleven."

"You said noon."

"Stay flexible, Tovah."

A few minutes before eleven the next morning Tovah waited outside the building. She wore a dress that was maybe too chic, especially given the bleached-out T-shirts she favored at school, but after Dezzy went to bed, there'd be some spare hours to relax in a beautiful apartment. She thought she'd do it in style.

She knew she'd never be back after today. Since the phone call, she'd been mortified by her matrimonial fantasy. You think you know yourself, the world. You believe you've got a bead on everybody else's bullshit, but what about your own? She'd had delusions of using this man because he somehow deserved it. Now she wondered if she even deserved to watch Dezzy. At eleven she pushed the buzzer. The elevator, just as Tovah remembered, opened into the plum-colored foyer.

She felt the hand on her shoulder even while asleep, and the whole day whizzed through her, all the games and snacks, the walk to the park, the Winnie-the-Pooh books, the TV programs full of anxious furry creatures, the sudsy bath, the creamy noodles, Dezzy's kissy snuggle at tuck-in. Tovah had come to the study afterward to read. The leather Eames had pulled her into sleep better than a pill. She blinked up at Mr. Gautier. He smiled, and his eyes looked fogged. His bow tie hung limp around his collar. His tuxedo took on a rumpled sheen in the lamplight.

"Wake up, little Toh-Va, wake up," he sang.

"Mr. Gautier." Her voice sounded deeper, liquored, in her ears. Her ears seemed stuffed with silk.

"How was your evening?" he asked. He sat on the coffee table beside her.

"It was perfect. How was your evening with the muckety-mucks?"

"Actually, I lied about the event. I don't know why. My older son got married today. Evan. He's a lawyer, she's a doctor. They will be very happy or something."

"Sounds ominous."

"No. They'll thrive. It's just been a long, emotional day."

"Was your ex-wife there?"

"Like I said, an emotional day."

Mr. Gautier stood.

"Drink?"

"I should go."

"You should have a drink with a sad old man first."

Mr. Gautier fetched Scotches from the kitchen, handed her one, and lowered himself on the arm of her chair.

"Is that comfortable?"

"It's an Eames ream," he said, laughed, stroked the back of Tovah's neck.

"What are you doing?"

"Tovah, let's be realistic. You're not the high school baby-sitter. I don't play bridge with your father. We're grown up and broken, just like everybody else. Stop acting like a precious flower."

Tovah set her drink down on the coffee table, rose, squeezed past Randy Gautier. She walked over to the bookshelf and stared out the window at the lights of the avenue, the darkness of the park. She pictured wolves, packs of them, leaping the gates.

"You know," she said, gathered herself. "It's very hard. Here. In America. In the world. For women. It's a fucking nightmare. Our choices are no choice. Everybody has a goddamn opinion, but nobody ever wants to help. The politicians, the culture, they push the idea of family, the importance of the mother, and they also push the idea of opportunities for women, but they screw us all on the stuff that counts, that will make it real. We are alone and suicidal or we have children and are suicidal. The only women who escape this are the rich. All the accomplished women in history had servants.

I'm convinced of that. Even if it's not true. It certainly feels fucking true. I'm sorry. I'm babbling. Why am I going on about this? It's stupid. I'm just cranky. Must be getting my period, right? That what you think? Well, fuck you, and of course I am. But that's not it. Maybe I wasn't ready to wake up just now. Maybe I'm tired of waking up. Nothing changes when I do. Nothing ever suddenly . . . Christ, I'm sorry. I should just go. Maybe I should just . . ."

Tovah turned and saw that Mr. Gautier had tugged his penis out of his tuxedo pants. He gave a shrug and, like a loved boy, beamed.

"It's okay," he said. "I'm listening."

the
DUNGEON
MASTER

The Dungeon Master has detention. We wait at his house by the county road. The Dungeon Master's little brother, Marco, puts out corn chips and cola.

Marco is a paladin. He fights for the glory of Christ. Marco has been many paladins since winter break. They are all named Valentine, and the Dungeon Master makes certain they die with the least amount of dignity.

It's painful enough when he rolls the dice, announces that a drunken orc has unspooled some Valentine's guts for sport. Worse are the silly accidents. One Valentine tripped on a floor plank and cracked his head on a mead bucket. He died of trauma in the stable.

"Take it!" the Dungeon Master said that time from behind his laminated cardboard screen. Spit sprayed over the top of it. "Eat your fate," he said. "Your thread just got the snippo!"

The Dungeon Master has a secret language we don't quite understand. They say he's been treated for it.

Whenever the Dungeon Master kills a Valentine, Marco runs off and cries to their father. Doctor Varelli nudges his son back into the study, sticks his bushy head in the door, says, "Play nice, my beautiful puppies."

"Father," the Dungeon Master will say, "stay the fuck out of my mind realm."

"I honor your wish, my beauty."

Doctor Varelli speaks like that. It's not a secret language, just an embarrassing one. Maybe that's why his wife left him, left Marco and the Dungeon Master, too. It's not a decent reason to leave, but as the Dungeon Master hopes to teach us, the world is not a decent place to live.

Now we sit with our chips.

"If they didn't say corn, I wouldn't think of them as corn," says Brendan.

He's a third-level wizard.

"Detention?" Cherninsky says. He stands, squats, sits, stands. He's got black bangs and freckles, suffers from that disease where you can't stay in your chair.

"He chucked a spaz in Spanish," I say. "I heard one of the seniors."

"The teacher rides him," Marco says. Marco despises the Dungeon Master but loves his brother. I like Marco, but I'm no fan of Valentine. I'm a third-level ranger. I fight for the glory of me.

The door smacks open.

"Ah, the doomed." The Dungeon Master strides past us, short and pasty, with a fine brown beard.

He sinks down at the desk behind his screen, which on his side has all the lists and tables for playing printed on it, and on our side has a mural full of morning stars and fire. We've been ordered never to touch the screen. We never do, not even when he's at detention. The Dungeon Master shuffles some papers—his maps and grids. Dice click in his stubby hand. Behind him, on the wall, hang Doctor Varelli's diplomas. The diplomas say he's a child psychiatrist, but he never brings patients here, and I'm not sure he ever leaves.

"When last we met," the Dungeon Master begins, "Olaf the thief had been caught stealing a loaf of pumpernickel from the village bakery. A halfling baker's boy had cornered our friend with a bread knife. Ready to roll?"

"I don't want to die this way," Cherninsky says.

Cherninsky always dies this way—we all do, or die of something like it—but he seems pretty desperate this afternoon. Maybe he's thinking of people who really have died, like his baby sister. She drowned in the ocean. Nobody ever mentions it.

"This situation begs the question," the Dungeon Master says, sips from a can of strawberry milk. "Is bread the staff of life or the staff of death?"

"What does that mean?" Cherninksy says.

"Read more. Enrich yourself."

"We all read," Brendan says.

"I mean books," says the Dungeon Master. "I can't believe you're a wizard."

"Don't kill me in a bakery," Cherninksy says.

"Don't steal bread."

"What do you want? I'm a thief."

"Roll."

Cherninksy rolls, dies, hops out of his chair.

"So why'd you get detention?" he says.

"When did I get detention?"

"Today," I say. "You got it today."

The Dungeon Master peers at me over his screen.

"Today, bold ranger, I watched a sad little pickpocket bleed out on a bakery floor. That's the only thing that has happened today. Get it?"

"Got it."

I know that he is strange and not as smart as he pretends, but at least he keeps the borders of his mind realm well patrolled. That must count for something.

"Now," says the Dungeon Master, "any of you feebs want to take on the twerp with the kitchen utensil? Or would you rather consider a back-alley escape?"

"Back-alley escape," says Marco.

"Valentine the Twenty-seventh?" the Dungeon Master says.
"Twenty-ninth."
"Don't get too attached, brother."

There are other kids, other campaigns. They have what teachers call imaginations. Some of them are in gifted. They play in the official after-school club.

"I've got a seventeenth-level elf wizard," Eric tells me in our freshman homeroom. "She flies a dragon named Green Star. We fought an army of frost giants last week. What about you?"

"We never even see a dragon, let alone fly one. You have a girl character?"

"You play with that psycho senior, what's-his-face."

"The Dungeon Master," I say.

"He calls himself that? Like it's his name?"

"He doesn't call himself anything."

"I heard that when he was little, he hit some kid with an aluminum bat. Gave him brain damage."

"Completely made up," I say, though I'm pretty sure it's true. "He's very smart."

"He's not in gifted," Eric says.

"Neither am I."

"Good point," Eric says, turns to talk to Lucy Mantooth.

Most days we play until we're due home for dinner. But sometimes, if we call our houses for permission, Doctor Varelli cooks for us—hamburgers, spaghetti—and if it's not a school night, we sleep over. Breakfast brings waffles, bacon, eggs, toast.

"Eat, eat, my puppies."

We puppies eat in the study. Since we die so often, we take breaks while one of us rolls a new character.

One day, while Marco makes Valentine the Thirty-second, I wander out to the parlor. Doctor Varelli sits on the divan with a shiny wooden guitar. His fingers flutter over the strings, and he sings something high and weepy. He stops, looks up.

"It's an Italian ballad." There is shame in his voice, but it's not about the song.

I follow his gaze to an old photograph on the wall. A young woman poses beside a fountain. Pigeons swoop off the stone rim. Marco once told me that this woman is his mother.

"So beautiful," I say.

"Of course," Doctor Varelli says. "Rome is a beautiful city."

Later, we gather in the study for a new adventure. Our characters join up at the Pinworm Inn. We've all died here before, in brawls and dagger duels, of poisoned ale, or infections borne on unwashed steins. But the Dungeon Master insists the place has the best shepherd's pie this side of the Flame Lakes.

We befriend a blind man. Cherninsky steals his silver, but the poor sap does not notice, so we befriend him some more. He tells us of a cave near the top of Mount Total Woe, of a dragon in the cave, a hoard beneath the dragon.

"Sounds dangerous," says Marco.

"That's the point," I say.

"It's a tough decision," Brendan says. I barely know Brendan. He met Marco at swim club or something. He's nice, kind of dim. Wherever he goes to school, I doubt the bullies even notice him.

Not true of Cherninsky. He makes a habit of asking for it, though some tormentors hang back. There's something wrong and a little sickening about him in the schoolyard. You sense he might take a bully's punches to the death. He's the kid people whisper has no mother or father at home, but of course he does, they're just old and stopped raising him years ago, maybe when his sister drowned. He always plays a thief, and even outside of the game, when he's just Cherninsky, he steals stuff from the stores on Main. He and the Dungeon Master are not so different, or this town hurts them the same, which is probably why they pick on each other.

"Damn it, Brendan," Cherninsky says now. "A tough decision? I say we go to that cave and get the gold. And then we get wenches."

"Wenches?" Brendan says.

"Tarts," Cherninsky says. "Elf beaver."

It's all a charade because there is no decision. There is no alternative. We shall scale Mount Total Woe or die trying. Most likely the latter.

"We're going to grease that dragon," I say.

"Grease?" Brendan says.

"Vietnam," I say.

"Oh, right."

But now the Dungeon Master has a mysterious appointment, which Doctor Varelli leans in to remind his beautiful puppy of, and the game adjourns.

Cherninsky and I head home. Soon we're near the reservoir. We squish ourselves under the fence. We stumble down a rock embankment and start throwing things into the water, whatever we can find—rocks, bottles, old toys, parts of cars. We've all grown up doing this. I guess it's our child psychiatry.

Cherninsky drags a shredded tire toward the shoreline. He waves off my offer to help.

"So what's your opinion?" he asks. "Think this Mount Woe thing is going to be any different?"

The tire wobbles in the water, pitches over with a splash. I whip a golf ball at its treads.

"Maybe," I say. "It could be."

"Saddest thing is how Marco and Brendan are so scared of dying. It's just a game, but he's playing with their minds. He's been to Bergen Pines. Did you know that? Certified mental. I'm quitting. This is a game for dorks, gaylords, and psychos, no offense."

"None taken," I say, though almost all of it is taken.

"Want to smoke weed?" says Cherninsky, claps my neck.

"No thanks."

"Want to watch my neighbor take a shower? She usually does it around now. She takes care of herself in there."

"What do you mean?"

"You know what I mean. Oh, forget it. You want to start a band? I have all the equipment."

"Where'd you get the equipment?"

"Don't worry about that. We'd need a name."

"How about Elf Beaver?"

"That's pretty stupid," Cherninsky says. "The fact that you thought of that could be a sign you're a nimrod. Help me with this other tire."

We eat leftover London broil from my mother's last catering job. My father, home from human resources, has his home-from-work work shirt on. He slices cucumbers for the cucumber salad, his specialty, while my mother pulls a tray from the stove. Upstairs, my sister squeals. She's all phone calls and baggy sweaters.

Today my ranger nearly got the snippo. A giant warthog jumped him in the woods. Is there even a warthog in the game manual? My ranger—his name is Valium, just to tease Marco—cut the beast down but lost a lot of hit points. Even now I picture him bent over a brook, cupping water onto his wounds.

Later he rests in the shade of an oak. The warthog crackles on a spit.

"How's it going over there?" my mother asks.

"Here?" I say. "Great."

"Awesome," my sister says, joining us. "Dead cow. Is there anything veggie?"

"Cucumber salad," my father says.

"Way to experiment with new dishes, Dad."

"Way to employ sarcasm," my father says.

"Not here," my mother says. "There."

"Where?" I say.

"The Varelli house."

"It's going fine," I say.

"Is it fun?" my mother asks. "I want you to have fun, you know."

"Yeah, it's fun, I guess."

My mother gives my father one of those meaningful looks that mean nothing to me yet.

"What?" I say.

"The Varelli kid," my sister says. "Isn't he the one who flashed those girls at the ice rink? And set his turds on fire in the school parking lot?"

"That was a long time ago," I say.

"It was kind of cool," my sister says. "In a pervert way."

"Poor Varelli," my father says. "His wife."

"That's the thing about it," my mother says.

"The thing about what?" I say.

My father turns to my sister and me as though he had something to say but has forgotten it.

"I put something special in the cucumber salad. Can you taste it?"

"Veal?" my sister asks.

"I've got nothing against you having fun and using your

imagination," my mother says. "But it's just too crucial a time to get sidetracked with games. And this one's a little scary. They write those articles about it."

"My grades are good," I say.

"It's middle track, honey. Of course your grades are good. But we're trying not to be middle-track people."

Later my father and I do the dishes, scour the pans—our pans, the catering pans.

"Don't worry," he says. "Everything will be okay."

Maybe he's that guy at the office, too—the reassurance dispenser, the diplomat. The middle man with the middle-track son.

"Are you guys getting a divorce?" I ask for no reason.

"Funny you should say that."

My father inspects the sudsy platter in his gloved hand.

"Yes," he says finally, "we are getting a divorce."

I stand there a stunned moment, until his weird, chirpy laugh kicks in.

"Gotcha!"

He must be the human resources jokester, though maybe I had it coming. Now he gets serious. My mother's catering gigs keep drying up and the raise he was counting on has fallen through.

My sister and I, my father says, will have to find after-school jobs if we mean to keep ourselves in candy and movies and music.

"There's still some time," he says. "Enjoy your game. We're just saying you might want to find some better things to do while you can. You're going to be plenty busy."

I don't really have better things to do. I could do what I did before I started going to the Varellis'. I could come home and eat too much peanut butter and hide in my room. I could lie in bed and think about Lucy Mantooth, toss a batch, nap until

dinnertime. I could watch TV and fake doing my homework.
But I'm not sure those are better things.

We tramp past the tree line of Mount Total Woe, reach a
stony ridge shrouded in mist. We hear odd bleats on the wind,
and our weapons are wet with the blood of minor beasts
we've slain along the trail. Deathbirds squawk overhead. Valentine the Whatever scans the rock face for possible points of
ingress.

It's hard to see far in the mist.

"I could weave a spell to clear it," Brendan says.

"What if the goats are shape-shifters?" Cherninsky says.

"What goats?" Brendan says.

"Those are goats. Only goats bleat."

"Sheep bleat," Marco says.

"And anyway," Cherninksy says, "why should we believe
that blind guy at the inn?"

"I think he was chaotic good," I say. "I recognize my own
kind."

"I'm sure you do," Marco says.

Marco's character is lawful good. It makes for what you'd
call personality clashes. But today's game is too amazing to
waste bickering. We smite the fanged and scaly, stalk the untold
riches the blind man did, in fact, tell us about. Meanwhile, no
runaway oxcart smears us into the road. We are not nipped by
rabid squirrels. We do not succumb slowly, like one early
Valentine, to rectal cancer. This must be what the official
after-school game is like—gifted children dreaming up splen-
dors, not middle trackers squirming beneath a nutso's moods.

What has come over the Dungeon Master? He seems almost happy behind his screen.

"Brendan's spell works," he says. "The mist is clearing.

About a hundred yards further to the top you can see an out-cropping and the mouth of a cave. Guarded, yes, by goats."

"We're going into that mountain," I say. "I can't believe we are going into that mountain. Let's stove some heads."

"And get the gold," Cherninsky says.

"Stove?" Brendan says.

"He reads," the Dungeon Master says, and shoots me a grin so rare it's a benediction. I decide not to tell him I stole "stove" from a whaling movie.

Now we're at the cave mouth. The goats sing their goat songs and part at our approach. Valentine takes a prayerful knee.

"Enough," Cherninsky says. "You can blow Christ on the way out."

"Infidel," Marco says.

"I'm an atheist," Cherninsky says.

"There are no atheists in foxholes," says Marco.

"Where are all these foxholes? I live in a house."

"Hey," I say. "Can we go into the fucking cave now?"

We go into the fucking cave now. It's dark, and we light torches, listen to bats flap off. We hunch and shuffle through the tunnel maze. Putrid fiends lurk at every dead end. That's how you know it's a dead end: something that smells like rotten sausage pops up and claws at your eyeballs. This is what we've always wanted, the classy monsters, hydras and griffins, basilisks, giant worms. The thief and the wizard set traps and decoys, cast spells of misdirection. Valentine and Valium, that suddenly ferocious duo, berserk right in with swords of dwarven steel. We bash and slice. Creatures fall in quivering sushi-like chunks.

The Dungeon Master, he almost roots for us. He refrains from his dire lessons. We're already steeped in the dire. We want to stab beasts.

We turn a granite corner, and there, lo and behold, we behold him. The dragon lounges, obscenely, atop a great apron of stone, vermilion scales blazing. Rainbow flame flutters from his nostrils with each dozy breath. He regards us through the slits of his amber eyes.

The dragon's treasure spills out from beneath him on the floor—gold, silver, rubies, jade. Just what's heaped around our feet at the threshold of the chamber is a princely sum.

"Let's take that," Cherninsky says.

"Take what?" Marco asks.

"What's around our feet. Just scoop it up and run."

"Not fight the dragon?" the Dungeon Master asks.

"I like it," Brendan says. "That's strategy."

"The dragon could really kill the hell out of us," Marco, who will never learn, explains.

"No. Let's fight the dragon," I say, and the Dungeon Master nods. "It's part of the game. Maybe we can tame him and ride him."

"Ride him?" Cherninsky says. "Are you out of your mind?"

"People do it."

"It would be cool," Brendan says.

"I got one thing to say," Cherninsky says, out of his chair now, pacing. "I'm not going to die here."

"Take a chance," I say. "Otherwise it's just boring. You're the one who said we shouldn't be afraid to die."

"When did I say that?"

"Down at the reservoir."

"The reservoir," the Dungeon Master says. "You guys talk about the campaign down there? You suck each other's little bird dicks and talk tactics?"

"Yeah," Cherninsky says. "We suck them Bergen Pines style."

"Guys," I say. "Stop it. Come on. Let's decide about the dragon. You really want to bail?"

"Better safe than sorry," Marco says.

"Is that an old paladin saying?"

"You're outvoted," Cherninsky says to me.

"Fine."

"Okay," Cherninsky says to the Dungeon Master. "We'll just scoop up what's near our feet and not rile the dragon. Can you roll for not riling the dragon?"

"Sure you want to do this?" the Dungeon Master asks. "This moment might never come again."

"We're sure."

"Listen," the Dungeon Master says. "I know I've been hard on all of you. I want to be more easygoing from now on. I want you to have fun."

"This is fun," Brendan says. "Really. Thank you. This is so exciting. But I think right now we should just grab a little gold and leave the cave."

"This is pathetic," I say.

"You don't know anything about real violence," Brendan says.

"What?"

"You heard."

"It's a dragon, man! It's not real!"

I notice Cherninsky slide a scrap of paper over to the Dungeon Master. The Dungeon Master drops dice in his leather cup, the one reserved for the most fateful rolls. The dice thump on the desk blotter.

"Consider the dragon officially riled."

"No," Brendan says. "No, no."

"Get the gold!" Cherninsky says.

I brandish my two-handed sword at the dragon while the others shovel treasure and flee.

"Come on!" they call.

"Go," I say. "I'll catch up. I've got a sudden craving for dragon burgers."

A smile wavers on the Dungeon Master's face. Because I am brave, I realize, he will spare me.

I charge the dragon, leap with my sword for his throat. Rainbow flame pours over my magic chain mail.

The Dungeon Master flicks his eyes at my roll.

"You're dead. Deep-fried."

"Huh?"

"A craving for dragon burgers? You think you're in a movie?"

"No," I say. "I think I'm in a fantasy game. And I have magic chain mail."

"Bogus magic chain mail," the Dungeon Master says. "You bought it off that wino monk."

"It's held up okay until now."

"You thought you could kill a dragon? Sorry, my friend. Long may we honor the memory of Valium."

"This is bullshit."

"Bullshit?" the Dungeon Master says. He's wound up. He really isn't that well. "It's not bullshit. It's probability. What, you gonna kwy? You gonna kwy like my little brutha? Life is nasty, brutish, and more to the point, it bites grandpa ass. Get it, bird dick? How's your two-handed bird dick now?"

"It's great," I say.

The remainder of the group makes it out of the mountain maze, but the goats turn out to be shape-shifters, just as Cherninsky warned. They transform into ogres with huge spiked maces. It's hardly a fight. Before he dies, Cherninsky's thief does manage to stick an ogre with his dirk. The ogre turns back into a goat, then into Cherninsky's dead sister, drenched, draped in seaweed.

"Just a little girl," the Dungeon Master says.

"You freak," I say.

Cherninsky's got his pen out, and I think he's about to go for the Dungeon Master's neck, but then he starts to bawl.

"Cry it out, sweetheart," the Dungeon Master says.

"Leave him alone," I say.

"This doesn't concern you," says the Dungeon Master. "Just back off. You have no clue."

"Okay," Marco says. "It'll be okay."

He sounds like my father.

"The hell it will," the Dungeon Master says.

The Dungeon Master holds up the note Cherninsky passed him.

"Wait till you hear this," he says. "Your pal was planning to steal everybody's gold. He wanted me to roll for it."

"He's a thief," I say.

"Go ahead, defend him."

"I am."

Brendan freezes in his chair. Cherninsky keeps weeping. Marco bobs in some ruined communion with the spirits of okay.

I stand, whack the screen off the Dungeon Master's desk, see the dice, the sheets of graph paper, the manuals and numerical tables. There are doodles on the blotter. Cross-hatched vaginas with angel wings. They soar through ballpoint clouds.

"I said never touch the screen," the Dungeon Master says.

"And I say don't flash girls you will never have at the ice rink. Don't set fire to your shits in the parking lot. You're a mental case. They should have kept you locked up."

The Dungeon Master comes around the desk, and I think he's about to make a speech. He lowers his head and spears me in the gut. We crash together to the floor. He squeezes my throat. I palm his chin, push. Marco screams, and I'm almost out of air when Brendan climbs the Dungeon Master's back, bites his head. They both tumble away. The door bangs open and Doctor Varelli leans in.

"Play nice, you goddamn puppies!" he howls, shuts the door.

We lie there, heaving. My wrist throbs. I smell raspberry soda in the carpet.

The Dungeon Master paws at the blood on his head. Brendan rubs his tooth.

"You children," the Dungeon Master says, rises, lumbers off. We hear him yell at his father in the kitchen. A loser, he calls Doctor Varelli, a lesbian.

"It's been a little difficult around here," says Marco.

I crawl over to the window. In the next yard, some kids kick a ball. It looks wonderful.

My broken wrist takes a long time to heal. I stay clear of the Varelli house, and at school only Eric signs my cast. He initials it, as though his full name might incriminate him. My dad says I don't have to get a job until the cast comes off.

I join the after-school club, roll a ranger called Valium the Second, but nobody thinks it's funny. Why would they? Lucy Mantooth plays a wizard-thief. It's clear she doesn't want me in the club.

Eric lives near me, and sometimes we walk home together. He likes to cut through some trees near the Varellis' house, but I never speak of them. One day we see the Dungeon Master's Corvette in the driveway. His father bought it for him last year, but the Dungeon Master has never driven it. He doesn't even have a license.

"You like our game so far?" Eric asks.

"It's cool."

It is cool, despite the death stares from Lucy Mantooth. We fly dragons, battle giants, build castles, raise armies, families, crops. But it's all too majestic, really. No goblin child will shank you for your coin pouch. You'll never die from a bad potato. I miss the indignities.

"I think Lucy likes you," Eric says.

"What's the giveaway? The fact that she never talks to me or that she rolls her eyes whenever I say anything?"

"Both."

"I guess I don't know much about girls."

"You'll learn," Eric says. "You've been out with those weirdos."

"Everything's weird if you look long enough," I say.

"I don't know about that," Eric says. "We're sponsored by the school, just like the chess team."

I get bored with Eric's game. Lucy Mantooth never warms up. Her wizard-thief leaves me for dead in a collapsing wormhole. Was there something I was supposed to say? I resume my old routine: peanut butter, batch, nap.

One day I'm headed home to do just that. A sports car pulls up to the sidewalk, a midnight-blue Corvette.

"Need a ride?" the Dungeon Master says.

I don't, but slide in anyway. I've never been in a Corvette.

We drive around town for a while, past my school, the hobby shop.

"Thought you didn't have a license," I say.

"Who said I do?" The Dungeon Master smiles. "There are rumors and there is the truth, and there are true rumors. You want the rundown? Here's the rundown. Hit a kid with a bat and gave him brain damage, yes. Flashing, yes. Burning my bowel movements, no. Have I been to the bughouse? I've been to the bughouse. Am I insane? Does my opinion even count? Remember all the newspaper stories about how the game makes kids crazy? Makes them do horrible things?"

"My mom clips them for me."

"Love those. Take, for example, suicides. The game doesn't create suicides. If anything, it postpones them. I mean, the world gives you many reasons to snuff it, got to admit."

"I'm fourteen," I say. "I don't know what I admit."

"In another age you could be a father already. In another neighborhood."

We drive for a while. We're a few towns east.

"Nobody's seen you lately," the Dungeon Master says. "Marco says you play with some snotty faggots at school."

"I stopped."

"You hear about Cherninsky? He got caught with all this stolen musical gear in his garage. Amps and guitars and drums, the whole deal. Tried to dump it in the reservoir, but the cops got most of it. Now his dad might go to jail."

"His dad?" I say.

"Harsh, right? Anyway, we're into war-gaming now. Real technical shit. It's not the same. Brendan can barely handle it. We're doing Tobruk. I'm Rommel."

"The Desert Fox."

"You read," the Dungeon Master says, though I picked up the name from an old tank movie. "That's what I like about you. That's why I thought I could teach you."

"Teach me what?"

We pull into a scenic lookout, the Palisades. Past the bushes in front of us the cliff drops sheer to some rocks in the Hudson. The Corvette idles, and I wonder if I made a mistake when I accepted this ride. The Dungeon Master looks off across the river, as though ready to jump it.

"Teach me what?" I say.

The Dungeon Master guns the engine. I turn to him, that pale skin, the fine-spun beard, the bitter, glittering eyes.

"Teach me what?"

His answer is another rev. His fingers drum on the gear

knob. We're going to fly a dragon after all. Part of me is ready. Maybe it's the part that kept me in Doctor Varelli's study so long. I grip my seat and await ignition, fire, scorched ascent.

"Damn." The Dungeon Master laughs. "You're shaking."

He shifts into reverse and swings the car around. Soon we're back on town streets.

"Had you shitting," he says.

"You did."

"I'm doing that for real at some point."

"Oh," I say.

"But not for a while."

"That's good."

"My dad's kicking me out after graduation. I think it'll be better for Marco. Kid needs to bloom."

"Where will you go? Your mom's house?"

"My mom doesn't have a house. She died when Marco was born."

"Really? I'm sorry. I figured she just left."

"Well, guess it's true in a way. No, I've got a cousin in Canada. We might room together."

"That'll be fun."

"Probably not. Here we are."

"Thanks for the lift," I say.

"You were almost home when I picked you up."

"Still, thanks."

I'm cutting across the yard when the Dungeon Master calls my name.

"No hard feelings, okay?"

I stop, picture him there behind me with his ridiculous head sticking out of the passenger-side window, but I cannot turn around. I'm still trembling from the drive. Do I have an almost uncanny sense in this instant of what's to come, some cold, swirling vision whose provenance I do not comprehend but in which I see the Dungeon Master, blue cheeked, hanging by his communion tie in Doctor Varelli's study, and Cherninsky, his dad in prison, panhandling with the scrawny punks, the pin-stuck runaways in Alphabet City, or me, Burger Castle employee of the month for the month of October, degunking the fry-o-lator in the late-autumn light?

Of course I don't.

"Really," the Dungeon Master calls again. "No hard feelings."

It must be the dumbest thing he's ever said. No hard feelings? What could ever be harder than feelings?

I want to tell him this, but even as I turn back, the Corvette peels away.

DENIERS

Trauma this, atrocity that, people ought to keep their traps shut," said Mandy's father. American traps tended to hang open. Pure crap poured out. What he and the others had gone through shouldn't have a name, he told her friend Tovah all those years later in the nursing home. People gave names to things so they could tell stories about them, goddamn fairy tales about children who got out alive.

Mandy's father, Jacob, had never said anything like this to Mandy, not in any of his tongues. He'd said other things, or nothing at all. He had worked for thirty-nine years as a printer in Manhattan. The founders of the company had invented the yellow pages.

"Think about that," he often said.

Mandy did think about it, the thick directory that used to boost her up on her stool at the kitchen counter.

She'd spent her childhood mornings at that counter, culling raisins from her cereal, surveying the remains of her father's dawn meal, his toast crusts, the sugared dregs in his coffee mug. Sometimes she wondered if he would come home from work that day, but it was a game, because he always came home. He'd eat his dinner and take to his reclining—or, really, collapsing—chair, listen to his belly gurgle, read popular histories of the American West, maybe watch a rerun of *Hogan's Heroes*, the only show he could abide.

His intestinal arias mostly stood in for conversation, but some evenings he managed a few words, such as the night he spotted Mandy's library book on the credenza. This teen novel told the story of a suburban boy who befriends an elderly neighbor, a wanted Nazi. Mandy watched her father study the book from across the room. The way he handled it made her think he was scornful of its binding or paper stock, but then he read the dust flap, shuddered. He whispered in his original language, the one he rarely used, so glottal, abyssal.

"Daddy," she called from the sofa, her leotard still damp from dance. She liked the way the purple fabric encased her, the sporty stink.

"Daddy," she said.

He spat out a word that sounded like "shame" but more shameful.

That night, her mother, who'd grown up in the next town over, who'd dreamed of exotic travel only to live her adventure on home soil—the older European man, handsomely gaunt, haunted, roaring up on his motorcycle at a county fair—commanded Mandy to explore new reading topics. The great explorers, perhaps. The not-so-great explorers.

"He never talks about it," Mandy said.

"There might be no words, honey."

"Does he talk to you?"

"We communicate," said her mother.

"Was he like this when you met him?"

"Yes. But it was different. He wanted to kiss me all the time."

Mandy decided she wouldn't read anything else about the era of her father's agony. If he judged her not good enough to hear his story, so be it. She'd await other, more generous catastrophes.

.

Like, for instance, the spring day a dashing fellow in a pink blazer knocked on their door. The man worked for Shell Oil, which wanted to build a new gas station down the block. Mandy, soon to turn eleven and annoyed by any news unrelated to her birthday party, had heard murmurings. The plans called for a monstrous sign, the glowing sort more suitable for the highway, and the neighborhood had mustered for a fight. The shop owners and the old Dutch families had joined with the doctors and lawyers to battle a common nemesis whose garish sign would pillage property values.

Lawrence, with his sailing tan and smart, maybe more off-salmon blazer, had been sent to talk to the townspeople—with honesty and understanding, he told Mandy's mother—about their misguided fears and the benefits of both the gas station and the sign, which, incidentally, would spin with incandescent beauty against the north Jersey night.

Alone, Mandy's mother let him in, and within an hour she agreed to assist him in his campaign. Within a week they were tearing off each other's polyfibers at Arlen's Adult Motel near the George Washington Bridge. Mandy heard the details years later from her aunt Linda, who added odd touches, such as Mandy growing a potbelly from too much junk food, since the assignations left her mother no time to cook. Mandy didn't remember that. She'd once seen Lawrence hunched over some papers in their kitchen—he threw her a funny, rueful look—but she did not recall a season of Whoppers and strawberry shakes. Still, for all she knew, her torments with mirrors and the malnourished beauties of fashion magazines and even her esophageal tract, all of which she had come to call, after years of therapy and therapeutic coffee dates, her "body shit," might as well have been spawned from the high-fructose despair of those months.

The Shell-sign resistance movement grew raucous and

strong. When word leaked of Mandy's mother's collabora-
tionist stance, somebody egged their stucco garage. Though
Lawrence's door-to-door sorties against the skyline puritans
seemed lonely and courageous to Mandy's mother, what tran-
spired was a legal contest between a smallish township and a
transnational corporation. The debate was bitter and point-
less, filled with the shouts of white men in wide ties. The coun-
cil zoned the lot for the gas station and the galaxy above the
lot for the sign.

Mandy's mother chilled champagne in the motel ice bucket,
but Lawrence never arrived for the victory toast. Not even
Linda knew if Mandy's mother drank the bubbly or poured it
over the terrace, but everybody remembered how she sobbed
herself home.

She clutched the motel's DO NOT DISTURB card for days.

Even Jacob seemed touched by his wife's distress. Who
could refute the awfulness of what this oil bastard had done to
the woman who once, long ago, after the Germans had murdered his mother and sister, had come reasonably close to being the only person Jacob could ever love. He tended to his wife
with the wary compassion of a plague nurse.

One night Mandy woke near dawn to see her father yanking open her bureau drawers. He stuffed a duffel bag with her
tank tops and jeans. She could count the times he had crossed
the threshold of her room, but now he scooped her in his arms,
as he'd once lifted their sick spaniel, Peppermint, slid her into
his sedan. She fell asleep again, cozy against the cool vinyl,
and woke once more in Linda's Upper West Side apartment.
Linda put a teacup to Mandy's lips. Her mother, they told her,
was dead. Running motor. Sealed garage. She'd left a note,
Mandy found out, years later, on a Shell petition in the kitchen.
"Oh, shit," it read. Beneath her scrawl, boldface words ex-
horted: "Give American Business a Chance!"

·

Her father was a survivor. Her mother had not survived. And Mandy?

Nineteen years later, Mandy was semi-surviving, had three months clean, some fluorescent key-ring tags to prove it. Her ex-boyfriend Craig had tags, too, wore them snaked together off his belt. Mandy saw him at the meetings, but she worried that he wasn't letting the program work on him, was maybe just white-knuckling it, a funny thing to say about a black man.

Craig had almost finished college before the pipe tripped him up. He possessed such a wry and gentle soul, except for the times he railed at her for being an evil dwarf witch who meant to stew his heart in bat broth (he'd majored in world folklore), and she'd always adored those horn-rimmed glasses that made him look like the professor he could still become. But if he had a discipline at the moment, an area of scholarly expertise, it was deep knowledge of how to steal electronics or lick diseased penises for the teensiest rocks. It wasn't as if Mandy had been any better months back. But now she was, and Craig, who often shared about what he called his terror runs, appeared to be planning one, the way some people contemplated a fishing trip.

Otherwise, things were on the uptick. Linda, in such pain these last few years, had gone to a better place. If an afterlife existed, Mandy figured that for Linda it would be more of the same—cappuccinos, Chinese, films at Lincoln Center. You could do that stuff dead. Now the studio apartment on a barren stretch of upper Broadway would be Mandy's. She deserved it—she had lived there as Linda's caretaker, never missed a medication or her aunt's chemo appointments, always laundered the sheets no matter how high she was off Linda's morphine.

Jacob spent his days in stoic near paralysis in a nursing home close to their old house, since sold to a happy (though you never knew) Sri Lankan family. Clean and sober, Mandy would be able to visit him regularly now. Also, Bill Clinton had been reelected, which was what Mandy had wanted, and perhaps most exciting, people were really responding to cardio ballet, the class she taught at the Jewish Community Center.

Maybe once she'd dreamed of jazz dance stardom, roses heaped on her Capezios, but keeping it real and teaching cardio ballet constituted triumphs enough. True, her sponsor, Adelaide, was in fact a star, a regular on the afternoon soaps, but that was just normal Manhattan recovery weirdness.

The main thing for Mandy was to focus on her goals and keep her eyes peeled for Craig. She could imagine the ease of a slip, a search for that early bliss when all they did was snuggle and drink brandy and smoke crack and have their soaring but oblique conversations about—about what, the vicissitudes? Was that the word Craig favored? Then they'd fuck and cuddle and twitch until dawn, whereupon the cooing of pigeons tilted them into jittery sleep.

But of course it went bad. You had to play the whole tape, Adelaide told Mandy from her makeup chair. Mandy's disease was just waiting for her to pick up again. Her disease was tougher than ever, did push-ups, Pilates. (The girl with the foundation paint nodded.)

"Remember those last, ugly moments," Adelaide said. "That's the part of the tape you've got to watch, Mand."

So Mandy remembered how their pigeon sleep scratched up their dreams, shattered their circadian clocks, which Mandy thought might also be their moral compasses. They fought, they hit—over drugs, money, presumed betrayals.

Most of the presumptions proved correct. Mandy confessed to mutual fondling with a banker from the rooms, a guy who liked to repeat the same story: how he got tired of always having to score and bought a half kilo for his apartment, but his cat found the package, clawed it to shreds—dead cat, toxic carpet, some unborn child's college education up in pharmaceutical-grade clouds.

"That pussy saved your life!" shouted a retired East Coast Crip in a wheelchair.

Uncle Drive-By, Craig called him.

While Mandy confessed her infidelity to Craig, she caught him eyeing the high-end Austrian cleaver on the magnetic kitchen strip. A good terror run begins at home. But they did a brave thing. They quit crack together, for the weekend.

Then came the day she entered the apartment, about a year after Linda had died, and through clots of rock smoke saw Craig, on his knees, his face in the crotch of an obese girl with a platinum chignon. The treasurer of Mandy's Saturday morning Clean Slate Meditations meeting jerked off in the girl's ear. Something about seeing the afghan Linda had wrapped herself in during her last, ravaged days shift under the girl's buttocks shook Mandy. Craig looked over, slurry eyed, asked Mandy to join the fun.

Yes, the vicissitudes.

Mandy summoned her inner banshee, threw a lamp, some decent flatware. The others fled, and Craig packed the measly possessions he'd amassed in his turd of a life—some rusted throwing stars, a box of stale marzipan, his crack pipe, his cherished coverless paperback edition of Knut Hamsun's *Hunger*—and scrammed. Now she saw him at meetings, tried not to retch at his conjob shares or recall the sweetness of their precious predawn hours, when addiction itself seemed as exquisite and harmless as a unicorn foal.

Today, after she'd led the ladies of cardio ballet through a quasi-sadistic grueler, Mandy leaned on the mirrored wall of the dance studio, sipped her bottled water, thought about her father in his living rigor mortis. If they'd had them when he was younger, he might have thrived in some sort of Holocaust support group, with sponsors, chips, key tags, coffee. Just once, history could have given her father a sloppy hug.

Mandy rolled her shoulders, sank into that honeyed post-class ache. A runnel of sweat curled down her calf. The day drained out of her. Endorphins filled her floodplains. Some people in recovery couldn't manufacture these chemicals anymore. But then her body tightened again. She sensed movement, a figure, a man maybe, tall, through the corridor window. The figure disappeared, and another, smaller person clopped toward her in chunky heels.

"You seem so peaceful, I hate to disturb you."

Tovah Gold looked twelve, but she had a degree in creative writing and a published poetry chapbook. She'd once presented a copy to Mandy but said she should not feel obligated to read it. Mandy sometimes wondered if Tovah thought she was dumb. The chapbook was called *For the Student Union Dead*, and Mandy thought the poems in it were dumb, the way smart people were often dumb.

Tovah taught a memoir class at the JCC. Mostly grandmothers spilling family matzo ball secrets, she'd said, or retired men composing disturbingly dry accounts of affairs with their best friends' wives.

"Mostly I just help them with their segues," Tovah once said.

"Hi," said Mandy now. "How's it going?"

"Horribly. No immortal lines this week, and my boyfriend,

or ex-boyfriend, I should say, has decided that our poetics are incompatible."

"Right there myself," said Mandy. "I kicked Craig out. He's bad for my recovery."

Tovah knew the Ballad of Craig and Mandy, took anthropological delight.

"What is it you all say?" she said. "Show up until you grow up?"

"Craig won't grow up. He can go to hell."

"But don't you think he needs some—"

"Girlfriend, please," said Mandy, did that dismissive wave all the sisters favored in meetings and lately on TV, but which Mandy couldn't master.

"What's that other one?" said Tovah. "You're only as sick as your secrets? Is that it? I love that one. It doesn't know it, but it's poetry."

"It knows it," Mandy said.

Tovah was a good friend, maybe her only one in the so-called civilian world, but that didn't mean Mandy couldn't hate her sometimes, the gooey earnestness that, along with the poetess shtick, seemed both pure and calculated, a saintly condescension. Tovah's innocence was a type of abuse. But Tovah's fondness for Mandy was genuine. That made it better and worse.

"Listen, Mandy," said Tovah. "I need to tell you something. I don't want you to feel strange about it. Because in my world, the artist's world, it's a common thing. But maybe not for normal people."

"I'm normal?"

"You're wonderful," said Tovah.

"Thanks," said Mandy, already mourning the rousing solitude of a few minutes earlier. Bitch had snatched her natural rush.

"Anyway," said Tovah, "I've been working on a poem cycle about you."

"A what?"

"A bunch of poems."

"About me?"

"Yeah."

"You don't know anything about me."

"I know a lot, Mandy."

"Not really. Maybe about me and Craig."

"Researching facts isn't the point," said Tovah. "It's about my construction of you. My projection."

"So," said Mandy, "I don't get it. Are you asking permission?"

"A real artist never asks permission."

"Oh."

"But I don't want any static between us."

"Am I Mandy?" said Mandy.

"Pardon?"

"In your poem, am I Mandy? Do you name me? Do you say Mandy Gottlieb?"

"No. It's addressed to a nameless person."

"Then why would I care?"

Tovah seemed stunned.

"Well . . . because it's so obviously you."

"But you said it's about your structure of me."

"My construction of . . . yes, that's right."

"So who cares?"

"I don't really understand your question."

"It's okay, Tovah. Write what your heart tells you to write."

"You are so marvelous, Mandy. You see life so clearly and simply, and it makes so much sense to you. I can't thank you enough."

"It's enough," said Mandy.

Tovah clutched her leather satchel, clopped away.

Mandy had a shower and steam, ran her favorite purple comb through her hair.

All you could do was stay clean and stay fit. Cardio ballet was mostly cardio. The ballet part was more like a dream of yourself.

Outside the locker room a tall man in a hooded sweatshirt leaned against the wall. He looked about thirty, with wavy hair and light stubble on his chin. His smirk seemed oddly familiar, almost comforting. Mandy made to move past him, and he cleared his throat, for comedic effect, she figured, though she could also hear phlegm swirl.

"Good class today?"

The man's voice was thin and kind.

"Do I know you? Have you taken cardio ballet?"

"I want to," said the man. "I want to very much."

"There's a sign-up sheet at the front desk."

"I was hoping to talk to you first. Get a read on the class."

"A read?"

"What it's all about," said the man.

"It's about cardio and ballet. Sign up. We need men."

"Would I get to be your partner?"

"Excuse me?"

"Your ballet partner. Throw you up in the air."

"Sorry. It's not very advanced ballet. This is just to get the blood pumping. There are other classes where you might . . . What? Why are you laughing?"

"I'm not laughing."

"You look like you're laughing."

"I know. It gets me in trouble sometimes. It's just how my

face goes when I'm listening to somebody kind and beautiful talk about something she cares about."

Mandy took a few steps back.

"Oh, no." The man palmed his mouth. "I guess I just accidentally spoke my heart! I should get out of here. I'm sorry. Maybe I'll sign up for the class."

The man grinned—tall, white teeth! You didn't see many of those in meetings.

At the table on the patio, overlooking a tomato field, her father picked at bird crap.

"Daddy," said Mandy. "That's poop."

Her father gave a lazy leer.

"How's your mother?"

"You know."

"Dead."

"How are you, Daddy?"

Jacob picked at the white shit flecks. "Never felt better."

An attendant came over, young, with cornrows, patted her father's arm. His printer's arm, shrunken.

"Having a good visit, Mr. Gottlieb?"

"Swell," said Mandy's father. It sounded like "svelte." He'd purged most of his accent nearly half a century ago, but now it crept back.

"I'm Mandy."

"Oh, I know," said the attendant. "I know all about you. He says sweet things about his Mandy. I take care of him."

"Does he ever talk about his childhood?" said Mandy.

"All the time. Sounds so special—upstate, fishing, and all that good stuff."

Mandy's mother had said something about a summer camp for war orphans in the Adirondacks. Jacob had been older than the other children, some kind of counselor.

Mandy noticed a glint in her father's eye now, some sour, annihilating shine. Mandy couldn't glean the source. The Nazi death machine? Shell Oil? The fact that only Mandy would remember him?

"Does he talk about the war? The camps? He never talked about it when I was a kid."

"What camps?"

"The one where soldiers bend you over and give you bread," said her father. "The one where you tell the guards where other men hide a rotten apple and they shoot those men."

"Maybe you should rest," said Mandy.

"But I have to get to the shop. Mr. Dwyer is expecting me."

"Better if you rest."

"Mandy, Mr. Dwyer's grandfather invented the yellow pages. What do you think of that? Ever have an idea like that? Your mother never visits. She still with the goy?"

"I want to thank you," said Mandy to the attendant. "For being here for him."

"It's my job."

"It's a noble job. I'd like to give you a little extra."

"Something extra would be appreciated."

"Mandy," said Jacob. "Darling. How's the whoring? You make enough money for the drugs? You let the *schvartzers* stick it in you?"

"Only one," said Mandy. "My fiancé, Craig."

She looked up to the attendant for some flicker of solidarity, got nothing.

Mandy dug in her bag, plucked some bills out, handed them over. The attendant tucked them into her pocket, but not before noticing, just at the moment Mandy did, that it amounted to only two or three dollars.

"Thanks," said the attendant.

"Goodbye, Daddy," said Mandy.

•

The tall man was not in cardio ballet the next week. Mandy did not think of him. She kept to her steps and turns, the ones whose flawless demonstration maybe merely mocked the panting people before her. Though she had known some of the women in the class for years, they all seemed a blur now, a slick, jiggling blob. Even as she glided into her Funky Pirouette, she thought, I need a fucking meeting. She'd been skipping them to avoid Craig. But now she decided to forgo her post-class musing-on-the-mats routine, head straight for the Serenity Posse II meeting on Amsterdam.

She shooed all that spandex and sadness out of the studio, switched off the lights, stepped into the corridor.

The tall man stood by the water fountain.

"I just came by to apologize for being a yammering idiot last week."

"No problem," said Mandy, "but I really have to go."

"Oh, okay, sure. My name is Cal, by the way."

"Mandy. I thought maybe you'd signed up for class."

"I'm afraid I'm not Jewish."

"You don't have to be Jewish to take an aerobics class."

"Are you sure?"

Mandy thought about it.

"I think anybody can join the JCC."

"Really?" said the man.

"Why not?" said Mandy. "But what do I know?"

"I guess it would be weird if you weren't Jewish, though," the man said.

He wore a scent, something for high school boys.

"Well, then," said Mandy. "I guess we better sneak you out of here."

"I thought you were going somewhere."

"I am."

•

It was just a nice neighborhood bistro and it was just a glass of chardonnay. She wasn't groping under a baseboard heater for a phantom rock. She wasn't sucking on a glass stem. Instead, she sipped from a stemmed glass. A slip, sure, her life was an endless slip, but this was civilized. This was civilization. Fuck crack. Fuck everything but chardonnay and Cal's teeth, his azure—which meant blue, but more intense, according to Tovah—eyes.

Cal lifted his glass.

"Mazel tov," he said.

"You mean *l'chaim*."

"No, mazel tov to you sneaking me out of there."

"Cheers," said Mandy.

"Are you Jewish on both sides?" Cal asked.

For a moment she thought he meant both sides of her body.

"Yes," she said.

"When did they come here?"

"Who?"

"Your people."

"I don't know. I think my mother's grandfather came from Holland or something. My father grew up in Europe. He came here and rode his motorcycle to the county fair. That's where my parents met. What about you?"

"Did your dad come after the war? Did he . . . was he part of the Holocaust? I mean, not in a bad way, I mean . . ."

"Yes, he was."

"Unbelievable."

"What?"

"No, just, it's so amazing he survived."

"It is."

"Because—I should just get this out there—I'm absolutely convinced all of that stuff really happened."

"I'm glad to hear it," said Mandy. This Cal was an odd bird. "What's your background?"

"I'm pure American," said Cal.

"So am I."

"No, of course you are," said Cal, studied the label on their wine bottle. Soon, Mandy knew, he would peel it.

"So, you're, like, a Jewish American."

"Hey," said Mandy. "What's going on?"

"I just like to get to know people."

"I see. Okay. Where are you from?"

"Oregon, originally."

"What brought you to New York?"

"A job. Computer stuff. I wanted to relocate. Change my life."

"I hear you."

"You don't like your life?"

"I take it one day at a time."

"Sounds reasonable," Cal said. The sopped wine label curled around his thumb. "You want to see a movie?"

"It's pretty late."

"Nah, it's early."

"I think the show times are over. I go to the movies a lot."

"We could go to my place," Cal said. "I have movies. I have a bottle of wine there. You like pinot blanc?"

"I don't know."

"Find out," said Cal.

"Next time," said Mandy. "I do have to go somewhere now."

Mandy ducked into the church basement, found a seat. There was something seriously off about Cal. She could picture him a king in the Middle Ages: Cal the Seriously Off. What a

waste of a slip. She didn't want to be here at the meeting, either, really, but some inner instrument had guided her. She
would never call it a higher power. Nor would she ever share
with booze in her system. You had to honor the honor code.

Adelaide waved, pointed to a free seat beside her. Mandy
shook her off. They all sat in the dark, dilapidated theater
built by the church during more enlightened years, when some
priest thought a sanitized production of *Hair* might lead bo-
hemian strays to Christ. Some nights it felt as though the
meeting were, in fact, an off-off-Broadway show, feverish, vital,
undisciplined. Now the addict audience nodded along with the
speaker, and when he'd finished, they took turns from the seats
with their woes. Newcomers bemoaned their cravings for pow-
ders, begged for release. Old-timers droned on about their sex
addictions, their divorces, how fat they'd gotten on red velvet
cake.

A familiar voice boomed from the back rows.

"I'm Craig, and I've got five weeks clean!"

"Hello, Craig!" answered the room.

"And I plan to make it this time, God willing, one day at a
time, but I don't feel safe right now, in the only place I can
ever feel safe, here with my Serenity Posse II posse. Why don't
I feel safe? Let me tell you a little story. Really, it's more like a
fable or a folktale. Once, long ago, this farmer worked his
fingers to the bone so his son could learn to be a warlock at
the castle. Every day the farmer's son walked many dangerous
miles to the castle for his classes, but one day a beautiful girl
stepped out onto the path holding a magic potion. 'Drink
this,' said the girl, 'and you will feel so fucking good.' Now
the farmer's son, truth be told, had dabbled in this kind of
potion before, but he knew it was wrong and had sworn off it.
This girl, though, she was so sexy, he figured, what the hell?
Well, I don't have to tell you the rest, do I? Except to say that

the beautiful girl turned out to be an evil skeezy witch who wanted to gobble up the farmer's son alive, which made the farmer's son act out in some emotionally hurtful sexual ways he couldn't control. The farmer's son did make amends to everyone involved, except the witch. He can't talk to the witch, because she's evil and contagious with spiritual cancer. Yet here she is tonight, the skank, testing me, testing me. You want war, bitch? Let's do it. Your lame, underdeveloped humanism is no match for my tower of higher power!"

Mandy rose, bolted up the narrow stairs toward the street. She could hear Adelaide scrape across the stone floor in her heels, but Mandy didn't look back.

She went home to vomit the wine.

The next night, after class, Cal stood in the corridor. He pointed his chin and she followed him out to the street. It felt like a music video.

Old movie stars stared out over the leatherette couch, the television, a rack of video cassettes, a card table with a few chairs. Mandy didn't get the old movie thing, but the posters looked classy in their frames. Gold trophies with karate guys obscured the dozen books on a lone shelf.

"Welcome to my humble abode," Cal said. He laughed, and Mandy decided the word "abode" made it funny.

The wine Cal brought from the kitchen was cold and a little tart.

"*Salud*," Mandy said.

"*L'chaim*."

They talked about whether they were hungry and decided to order something later. Cal ripped open a bag of that intelligent popcorn.

"So," he said. "What do you feel like watching? Something sad, something funny? A drama?"

"How about something romantic?" Mandy said, but Cal pursed his lips in a fretful way, and she regretted it. "Or a thriller!"

"I've got something," he said, tucked a tape into the slot.

Mandy knew what he'd chosen from just a flicker of it. It was black and white, but it wasn't old. She'd dragged herself to see this film after it won every award. She thought it might help her understand her father, but she'd left the theater after that sexy British actor kept shooting Jews from his balcony.

"I don't think so, Cal."

"What?"

"Not this. Let's watch something else."

"But this is the most important movie ever made. You can't even get this at the store. I have a friend who—"

"Please turn it off," Mandy said.

Cal paused it.

Any excuse could work. She just needed to get her jacket from the chair.

"It's heavy, I know," Cal said. "I've seen it dozens of times. I always cry."

"Why?"

"Why? How can you ask that, you of all people?"

"No. Why have you seen it dozens of times?"

"So I can understand," Cal said.

Now he stood, clenched and unclenched his fists. His arm veins twitched.

"So I can understand and get well," Cal hissed.

He stared at Mandy, and she tried to get a read, as he might have put it.

Just a beating, or a bonus rape?

But then Cal relaxed, or really kind of deflated. His breathing slowed, and he kneaded his hands.

"Man, I'm sorry."

"It's okay." The jacket would be easy now. But how many bolts were on the door?

"I need to tell you something."

"No, you don't," Mandy said. "It's all okay."

"I do," Cal said. "Because there is something good between us and I don't want to mess it up."

"Everything's fine."

"Six fucking million," Cal said. "How can it be fine?"

"Don't forget the Gypsies," Mandy said. "Millions of Gypsies. And gay guys. Union guys. Retarded people. Tons were killed."

"Six million Jews," Cal said.

"I know all about it. Is that what you wanted to tell me?"

"No," Cal said, and told her what he wanted to tell her. When he was done, he took off his shirt and showed her the tattoos, the swastikas and iron crosses and even an ingenious Heydrich who *sieg heil*ed when Cal flexed his deltoid.

"But you say you had no choice in prison," Mandy said. "It was the Brotherhood or get the skiv."

"The shiv. But no, Mandy. I believed it all. I was hard core. Even before the Brotherhood. That's how I got to prison. I beat a guy almost to death. I thought he was a Jew. Turned out he was something else. Probably would have hated him anyway. Do you get it?"

"Get what?"

"What I'm trying to do."

"Not really."

"I'm confessing my sins. To you. I want to get better."

"Are you even attracted to me?"

"Not in a healthy sense," Cal said. "I mean, I definitely went out of my way to find the cutest girl at the JCC."

"I'd better go."

"Please, Mandy. Stay."

"No."

"I've got other movies," Cal sobbed.

Home, Mandy found a message on her machine from the nursing facility. It was garbled because every message was garbled on this crappy old machine that Craig had stolen off a homeless guy's blanket and given to her with great ceremony on her birthday, but she thought she heard the words "mild" and "stroke." She'd have to wait until morning for a bus.

She called Adelaide.

"I knew you used," said Adelaide. "I could tell. What happened, honey?"

"I just had some wine."

"Just some wine? Who are you talking to, Mandy? Do you want to die?"

"Not tonight."

"Good girl. I'll have the car pick you up in the morning, take you to the soundstage. I've got a read-through, but after that we can hit a meeting. I have to say, I have a crazy week. You picked a fucked time to slip. But I've got your back."

"Thanks, Adelaide."

"Don't thank me too much. It'll go to my head and I might relapse!"

"My father had a stroke."

"Oh, Jesus, I'm sorry, sweetie."

"Maybe you could come out to the nursing home with me?"

"The one in New Jersey? Honey, you know I don't go out there unless somebody has died. Is he going to die?"

"They said mild."

"Mild is the best. Don't worry, baby. Call me whenever. I'll try to call back. No fucking wine, Mandy. Don't be a victim."

"Okay."

"What kind of wine?"

"Chardonnay."

"I'm not envious at all," Adelaide said.

Her sponsor hung up before Mandy could tell her about the pinot blanc.

Tovah answered Mandy's call on the first ring, as though waiting years for this moment.

"Of course I'll come with you," she said. "In fact, I have a car."

"I don't mean to impose."

"I would be honored," Tovah said.

A poem cycle.

Like what some stuck-up clown would ride.

Tovah's Subaru had a dead battery. The garage guy offered to jump the car. He popped the hood, and they all leaned in for a better look at the massive corrosion, the split hoses, what the garage guy called a cracked block. Not that Tovah could have known. She never used her car, had loaned it out often over the years.

"I'm still going with you," she said.

They didn't speak much during the bus ride. Tovah scribbled in her notebook, and Mandy studied the Hudson River and hated Tovah. They got off at the town plaza and bought some calzone.

When they reached the home, they found Mandy's father sitting up in his patio chair. Mandy had expected a weirdly folded arm, a contorted jaw, maybe some slobber, but he looked fine. He waved off the food but gestured for Tovah to join him. The attendant Mandy had tipped pulled her into a tiny dispensary to talk.

"So," Mandy said. "He seems pretty okay. Pretty . . . mild."

"The doctor was here this morning. We're thinking now it wasn't a stroke at all."

"That's great."

"Yeah, well."

"Well, what?"

"The doctor noticed some other things. Symptomatic things with the eyes and such. Your father described recent headaches."

"Headaches?"

"The doctor wants to run some tests."

"Tests for what?"

The attendant pointed to her temple, shrugged.

"What does that mean?" Mandy asked.

"Nobody knows anything. That's why we have tests."

Maybe if Mandy had tipped the attendant more, she would have divulged the ailment that would soon slaughter her father.

The attendant stepped out of the dispensary. Mandy paused before she followed. Craig would have known how to bang those white cabinets open, grab the goodies.

Tovah and Mandy's father hunched together at the table. Mandy joined them, started to think of something nostalgic and uplifting to say, when she realized she couldn't understand them at all. They spoke in what sounded like German about something very serious, but also occasionally funny, and frightening and unendurable, judging by Tovah's face, which every so often froze like the faces of women in silent movies.

"You guys are getting on like gangbusters," Mandy interrupted. "Tovah, I had no idea you spoke German."

"It's Yiddish. My grandmother taught me."

"What are you guys talking about?"

"The whatchamacallit," Jacob said.

He stared up at his daughter with that foul gleam. She'd never had a chance, really, could never be the daughter, the destiny you claw through the blood and feces of enslavement, of death, to claim. She consoled herself with something she'd read back in the days she still read about the whatchamacallit by the man who threw himself down the stairs: the good people died. Mostly only assholes made it out. That was how she remembered the passage anyway. That was her read.

"You must know all these stories," Tovah said.

"Yes, I'm a child of a survivor. A survivor of a survivor."

Mandy smiled, stood. "I need to check on some things. Are you two okay here for a while?"

"Oh, yes," said Tovah. "Your father is amazing. I had no idea."

"Daddy?"

"How's your mother doing?" he said.

"She's dead, Dad. Feel free to share your pain about it."

Jacob's cheeks drew in.

"You can't share pain," he said, put his hand on Tovah's wrist. "This girl knows that. She's a poet."

It took hours to cross the towns—Nearmont, Eastern Valley, Rodney Heights—that led to Mandy's old house. All that cardio ballet, and it still wiped her out, though she got her second wind and a floaty feeling in the bargain. Her friends, the endorphins. She wanted to leap off a boat and swim with them.

Now she stood at the end of the driveway on Duffy Lane, a lost pilgrim in front of the pea-green split-level with beige trim. She ached for a certain sensation, a sudden click in the soul's alignment. Closure, some called it in the meetings. The more churchy addicts referred to forgiveness, but she'd always known what people meant. She'd hungered for it.

Maybe if she just knocked on the door, the family inside would bid her welcome. She'd knock, and when a beautiful Sri Lankan boy answered, she'd lean down and whisper her story.

"Is it closure you seek?" he'd say in melodious English.

Inside, the father of the family would smile and take the mother's hand.

"You have made us happy by coming," he would say. "We have waited many years for this."

"Closure is not forgiveness," the mother would say, with even more melodiousness than the child. "But you are a blessed one, for you shall enjoy both."

Then there would be an unexpected crunching sound, but actually that noise wasn't coming from Mandy's movie. An SUV rolled into the gravel driveway. The doors opened and children scurried out in scout uniforms. A tired-looking woman with grocery sacks followed.

"Can I help you?" she said.

Mandy thought she might be Brazilian. Or maybe Belgian.

"Look," the woman said, and stabbed a finger down the road. "If it's about the nightclub, I already signed the petition. I don't want them to build it any more than you do. Those drunks will crash into my living room. But I'm really busy right now. Take care."

Mandy nodded, and the woman turned to her stoop.

Her legs throbbed, had gone rubbery, and the bus back to the city was in the other direction, but Mandy hiked on around a bend of firs. The Shell sign hovered, its colors dulled, a corner of it broken, or maybe bitten off. They'd shuttered the station, covered the pumps with dirty canvas hoods.

What the poor woman died for, thought Mandy, but then knew it was a rotten thought, too romantic, something for Tovah's poem cycle. The blazer, the tan, the lost dream of

American entrepreneurship, her seduction and abandonment by transnational loins—these things hadn't killed her mother. Nor had her father, with his smeary, world-historical wound. What murdered her was her mind, a madness factory full of blast furnaces and smokestacks. Mandy's mind had erected one, too, but Mandy would discover a way to raze it. She would grow a beautiful garden on the ashes of the factory, teach cardio ballet in more and more places, build a modest cardio ballet empire. She would forgive Craig and help him however she could. She would help everybody. She would save herself.

The bus pulled into Port Authority, and she rode the subway uptown. Cal waited near the door of her building, and again they didn't speak but did their dance of nods and shrugs, and he followed her into the lobby, just as he must have followed her home some night to know where she lived. What was creepy to civilians was protocol for their kind. How else were you going to figure out where somebody lived, where the drugs were, or the money, or somebody to cling to long enough to forget the shame.

Inside the apartment, Cal pulled a bottle of wine from his coat, but Mandy shook her head, poured them glasses of water from the tap. They gulped them down and filled the glasses again. Then Mandy led Cal into the bedroom and lit a lavender candle. Cal stood before her and stroked her hair.

He started to take off his shirt, but Mandy whispered, "No." He seemed to understand, even tugged his sleeves down to his wrists to better hide his tattoos. He pulled her to the bed, and his body was smooth and taut through his shirt. Toward the end, he whispered something too muffled to make out, though she heard the words "beautiful" and "feels" and "so good," and then maybe "cabal."

The world was what it was, one day at a time. Mandy

rocked Cal to sleep and thought about this day she'd had, this stranger in her bed. She thought about pinot blanc. She thought about all the colors of the key tags, about salmon and salmon-colored blazers and the cleaver on the kitchen's magnetic strip. Before she fell asleep, she yawned once and stretched her arm across the panzer tank, invisible to her now, that in the morning would burst forth in loud hues from Cal's belly.

Tomorrow she'd look up tattoo removal. They were doing big things with lasers. When he was just a little more stable, she'd break up with Cal, gently, and then she'd begin her project of helping everybody she could help, and after that she'd head out on a great long journey to absolutely nowhere and write a majestic poem cycle steeped in heavenly lavender-scented closure and also utter despair, a poem cycle you could also actually ride for its aerobic benefits, and she'd pedal that fucker straight across the face of the earth until at some point she'd coast right off the edge, whereupon she'd giggle and say, "Oh, shit."

the
REPUBLIC
of EMPATHY

WILLIAM

My wife wanted another baby. But I thought Philip was enough. A toddler is a lot. I couldn't picture us going through the whole ordeal again. We'd just gotten our lives back. We needed time to snuggle with them, plan their futures.

But Peg really wanted another baby, said we owed Philip a brother or a sister. That seemed like a pretty huge debt. What do you do for the second child? Have a third?

"Peg," I said. But I had no follow-up. Or was it follow-through?

Peg sat at the kitchen table scribbling in the workbook she'd gotten from Arno, her German tutor. The handwriting didn't look like hers, though I couldn't remember the last time I'd seen her handwriting.

"This is a dealbreaker," Peg said.

"The deal being our marriage?"

"Please don't leave me," she said.

"Who said I wanted to leave?"

"If you refuse to have another baby, that's the same as leaving me."

"This is emotional blackmail."

"The emotional aspect is implicit. You could just say blackmail."

"But why, Peg?"

"This morning I smelled the top of Philip's head. That sweet baby scent is gone. Now it just smells like the top of any dumbshit's head."

·

I took Philip for a walk. He tired easily, but his gait was significant. He tended to clutch his hands behind his back, like the vexed ruler of something about to disintegrate.

"How about a brother or a sister?" I asked.

"How about I just pooped," Philip said.

"Thanks for your input."

Peg always said I shouldn't model sarcasm for the boy, but who will? Everybody's so earnest around children. Besides, I've always wanted to model, to strut down the runway under all that strobe and glitter while the fashionably witty cheer on my sarcasm.

Later I had to jet over to the office. The flip-flop prototypes were a total joke. Art had ignored my notes. Where were the porpoise pods, the sea grass? I hated Art. They needed some attitudinal realignment, or whatever the badasses say. Art and I were scheduled to meet in the meeting room and communicate about our communication problems.

Gregory walked up to my desk. He didn't work for our company, but rented a room in the building, where he made paintings for plays and movies. Gregory painted to the specifications of the filmmakers and stage directors. He could paint a copy of a famous painting or create a whole original series to represent the work of a character in a play or a movie. His oeuvre wasn't known, but it had won fame and riches for fictional artists in several films.

Gregory always wore a festive shirt and a baseball cap with no logo. He said he wore these clothes because he believed they made him resemble a thoughtful, retired gay cop, which he was.

He'd come to see if I'd join him for a joint.

"Code Doob," he said.

"Stat," I said.

We went to the roof and smoked and stared at the large metal exhaust units mounted on nearby roofs.

"So, Peg . . ." I said.

"She wants to do a number two," Gregory said. "I mean . . ."

"Oh, yeah, I told you already," I said. "Guess I don't have anything super-recent."

"That's okay," Gregory said. "I got one. Guy just asked me to do a painting. Not a copy job, but a painting in the style of. A very famous painter. Died young, but did spectacular things. A great talent. All my gifts would fit in his pinkie, and so forth. This guy said he would pay me the equivalent of what I thought a real, newly discovered peak-performance painting by this painter would fetch. I said it would be many millions. He said, 'Fine.'"

"Why?"

"Said he's interested in exploring questions of authenticity, and he's got the money to do it. Investment banker. But did some art theory in college. He's not going to throw his money away on a yacht he'll have no time to . . . yacht on. Here, at least, he's shaking things up."

"You'll be so rich."

"I told him to go to hell."

"Why?"

"I'm a copyist and a hack visionary, but I'm not a criminal. Fuck the banker."

"You're a proud man," I said.

"If that's all it takes. Hey, look."

Across the way, on the roof of another building, two figures fought. They both wore dark coveralls and walkie-talkies clipped to their tool belts. They threw huge roundhouse punches, wrestled, choked each other, broke apart, and banged each other into the shiny exhausts and flues. You could hear the metal flutter.

"It's either about money or women," Gregory said.

"Or another man," I said.

"Don't get inclusive on my account," Gregory said.

"Shouldn't we call this in?"

"Good thinking, Citizen."

We did call it in, but only after the next thing that happened. One of the guys grabbed the other guy's shirt and spun him off the edge of the building. The falling guy fell. His head hit a steel fence post and made a moist, crunching sound. His body slid limp beside a Dumpster. Vomit fired up my throat. Gregory called it in, used a language I knew vaguely from television.

We gave statements to the police. Afterward we went to a bar. Gregory warned me that I might have nightmares about the grisly scene we'd just witnessed, but if I had the wherewithal to utter, from within the dream, the word "Miranda," I might break out of the gruesomeness.

"Why Miranda?" I asked.

"Oh, that's just what I use. You can use your own word."

"Was she a friend of yours, Miranda?"

"She's the friend of every cop who believes in a person's right to remain silent."

Peg was angry that I got home so late, but when I told her the story, leaving out the joint part, she seemed appeased. She didn't care if I smoked marijuana. She smoked it or, rather, took tinctures of THC on her tongue. But the idea that I might be out of the house doing anything enjoyable, and not generating revenue, enraged her. She had a right to be enraged. She was home with our son a good deal. It took a toll. You can cobble together a solid twelve minutes of unconquerable joy a day caring for a toddler. It's just the other fourteen or fifteen hours that strip your nerves and immolate your spirit. Peg was a warrior, but she got testy the time I told her that. She said she didn't want to be a warrior. She wanted to be the smart, sexy, sociable woman she'd been before Philip.

I should have said, "You are, honey. You still are."

Instead I said, "Better save up for a time machine."

We hardly talked for a week. But I guess she'd forgiven me, as lately it had been all about another baby, and today my absence had been excused, even if it took a corpse to clear the air.

"You must be traumatized," she said. "Oh, sweetie."

She sat on the carpet with Philip, who chewed on a toy hammer.

"I'm okay," I said.

I squatted down and stroked Philip's face.

"It just reminds you of the fragility of everything," I said. "Especially the fragility of brawling on the roof of a very tall building."

"Let's not ever do that to each other," Peg said, her eyes filling with tears.

That night, I dreamed I had another son, a bigger one, and he punched me in the neck and I stumbled off the edge of a skyscraper. I fell through the air. I could also feel myself climbing out of the dream. Gregory floated near me, waved.

"Miranda!" I shouted. "Miranda!"

Peg shook me awake.

One hand cradled my head, the other hovered in a fist.

"How long have you been seeing this Miranda?" she asked.

"She's a constitutional guarantee," I said.

"She goes all night?"

"Forget it."

"I can't," Peg said. "I'm pregnant."

"We're going to have a second kid? I thought we were going to keep discussing this."

"A second kid? We have two kids already."

"We do?"

Two boys walked into the room. One looked like Philip, but a few years older. The other, smaller, didn't look like anybody I knew. They wore matching airplane pajamas.

"We can't sleep," the Philip-looking one said.

"Come on down," said Peg, like a very tired game show host.

The two boys slid into bed with us. The smaller one curled up beside me. He giggled and put his finger in my ear.

"Papa," he said, dug hard with his fingernail.

"Ow!"

I jumped out of bed, clutching my ear.

"Toby," Peg said. "Don't hurt your father."

I ran out of the bedroom and into the living room. Things looked different in our dark apartment. I opened another door to step into the hall. But cool, spongy grass had replaced the smudged carpet. In fact, there was no hall. I stood on a lawn on a moonlit lane. Night air filled my lungs, and I stared up at the stars, then across to the houses, cream houses with high porticos that sat along the silent block. In one, flabby nude figures moved behind a blindless bay window. The goddamn Lockwoods masturbated each other on their sofa again, though how did I know their name or that these exhibitions were habitual? Did it matter? This couldn't go on. What if Philip, or the other one, what's-his-face, Toby, saw?

DANNY

Dad picks me up on Knickerbocker near the monument in Cresskill. He has his new girlfriend in the car. I throw my bag into the backseat and slide in, shut the door.

"This is my friend Lisa," Dad says.

"Totally sincere greetings," I say, stick my hand over the seatback. Lisa grins. She looks younger than Dad's last few. He goes through them quick—like he's stoked by the idea of them, but when they get too close, he has to send them packing. Or else, and this is my buddy Ronko's theory, he's secretly gay, and can't face it. But who ever heard of a gay homicide cop, and besides, there's no way you could be gay with this chick Lisa around. She has such nice, soft-looking hair, which is a tell-me-about-the-rabbits-George thing to say, but what can you do?

"Hi," Lisa says. "It's good to meet you. I've heard a lot of stories."

"I'm sure they're all true, but skewed by my dad's peculiar vision of the world."

"What's his vision of the world?"

"He thinks raccoons are advance scouts for alien invaders."

"It's clear from their behavior that they work for the Greys," Dad says.

"Oh, Gregory," she says, and gives his head a playful shove.

"Watch out, I'm driving here!" Dad barks.

"Hey, Lisa," I say. "What's the lamest car in Bergen County?"

"A gold Firebird with four on the floor."

She's a local girl. She remembers that nasty joke from years before, after a quartet of satanic metalheads turned their car into a carbon monoxide Jacuzzi and went to meet their master.

She's probably just a few years older than me.

"What are you two talking about?" Dad asks. He's no local boy. He's from Brooklyn. He moved us out here to Jersey when I was a kid. Dad's also old. Too old for this chick. But you have to hand it to him. I generally want to hand it to him, and then, while he's absorbed in admiring whatever I've handed to him, kick away at his balls. That's my basic strategy. Except he has no balls. Testicular cancer. Sounds like a bad rock band. I sound like the narrator of a mediocre young adult novel from the eighties. Which is, in fact, what I am. Exactly whose colostomy bag must I tongue wash to escape this edgy voice-driven narrative?

Back at the house, Lisa grills some steaks while Dad and I chop veggies for the salad.

"How's your mom doing?" he asks.

"Mom?" I say.

"Your mom," Dad says.

"Mom?" I say.

"Yes, Mom," says Dad. His serrated blade bites into the cutting board. It's like that commercial with the beer can, the tomato, the Japanese knife.

"Mom's fine," I say. "She's rimming this experimental bassoonist from Santa Cruz."

Dad throws the knife down, shoots me his photon-torpedo eyes.

Shields up.

"Don't you talk about your mother that way," he says.

"What?" I say. "I love the bassoon."

"You know what I mean."

"Sorry, dude," I say.

Shields hold.

"Steaks are almost done," Lisa calls from the deck. "Hope you like them severely wounded, but not dead."

"Fantastic!" Dad shouts back. He's got this big smile on his face, like he's happy or something. It's a rare expression. Mostly you only see it on the weekends, when he's working on his paintings. It's how he relaxes from being around so much homicide. Now his eyes flick my way, and I see that happiness drain away.

What Lisa just said, that's how I feel about my relationship with Dad: severely wounded, but not quite dead. Okay, maybe that's sappy and jervis, but it's how I feel, and as the young protagonist, my job is to keep you abreast of my feelings. I'm brash, but you better believe I hurt inside. Like I said, I will do windows and colostomy bags. Just get me out of here before I have to tell you in the next chapter how I think internal affairs is investigating my father, and what it's like to be the son of a cop, and also what it's like just to cope with all the strangeness in the world, strangest of all being that I just know, with a certainty I've never experienced, that before she is out of our lives forever, I will be in Lisa's ass, though you probably won't get to see it, or even hear me use the phrase "in Lisa's ass," because this book depends on school library sales.

LEON AND FRESKO

Leon banged open the metal door and staggered out onto the tar-covered roof. Fresko followed. They circled each other in sunlight, both men in a martial crouch. Voices screeched from the walkie-talkies on their hips. They wore shirts with name patches. Leon's said LEON. Fresko's said PETE. They worked maintenance in adjacent buildings. They were friends, and they planned to make an action movie with Leon's new camera over the weekend. During lunch they rehearsed the dialogue for the fight scene.

"One of us is going to die today," Fresko said.

"That would be you, dog," Leon said. "It's time to punch out, bro."

"I'll dock your goddamn existence."

"I'll take it up with the grievance committee."

"They'll be grieving for you," Fresko said.

"No time for arbitration, son. See this fist of mine? This is your severance package."

Leon and Fresko charged each other. They didn't know how to movie fight. They only knew how to fight fight. So, by tacit agreement, they fought fought. It was the only way the scene would seem real. They ran at each other, collided, punched. They kicked and bit and spun in a clinch. And then Leon fell off the side of the building. Fresko thought it was a joke. It didn't seem as if it was happening, but it was happening. That's how so many things happen.

You would never be able to ask Fresko about it. Not much later, he was doing five years for manslaughter. He hardly ever spoke, though one day he started to laugh and didn't stop for hours. Somebody on the cellblock asked him what was so goddamn funny, but he couldn't get the words out. What struck him at that moment was the realization that he and Leon had never solved the question of who was going to shoot the scene. They'd be too busy fighting, and there was nobody they could trust to do a decent job. Maybe the camera could have followed the action if they had used some sort of professional robotic thingamajig, but how could they have afforded such equipment? They were janitors, for God's sake. Oh, Leon. You moron. You were the only friend I ever had. We were going to be viral on the Internet. I didn't spin you hard. You let punk-ass physics take you. Together forever, I thought. But you had to be a pumpkin. You had to smush your dumbshit head.

ZACH

Even a monkey can make money. That's what my mother always told me, but I think she undersold herself. She was a remarkable woman. That's why I'm remarking on her now. She was also the only person who ever seemed like a person to me.

She started like everybody else, if everybody else started as a half-cultured girl from Connecticut who reckoned that all she had to do was sustain an aura of dazzling freshness and a husband would arrive to keep her in cozy bondage. She'd raise some love-starved children, and the husband would bring home the bacon and, with any luck, not spend many waking hours at home eating it.

This is exactly how it went for a while, but then her particular bacon procurer drove home from the city dead drunk and died. So she went out and made her own, well, let's just call it money again. My mother became a successful Realtor and invested early in many soon-to-be lucrative areas. But her stock market strategies aren't the point. The fact that here was a woman, a nearly destitute widow in a very sexist America who ventured out into a man's world and slayed, is the point. I grew up rich, and she sent me to top-shelf schools. I took art history and some art theory classes that puzzled and intrigued me. There was the funny lingo. Everybody was always "interrogating hegemonic discourse" and so forth. I hung out with kids who were really fascinated by this crap. They were also really into cocaine and sex. I was bound for an M.B.A. after college, but I liked to sit around the table late at night, drunk and high, smoking cigarettes and arguing points that I had just barely grasped in seminar. I usually brought the cocaine, and I was often rewarded with sex.

I forgot most of this for many years. I went into banking

and made mad cake. I managed a hedge fund and made madder cake, or, rather, money. I became one of those guys you never see and have never heard of but who is the sick-ass king of certain sectors of the market, employing instruments you could never in your math-illiterate lifetime comprehend. I know this tone, my tone, is insufferable. But that's the thing that nobody understands. If you want to make money, you have to be smart and a cunt and also work harder than anyone else. Most folks can't manage all three. But I could, and I prospered, as my mother had.

Then my mother died. It sucked in all the ways you'd be familiar with if your mother (assuming she wasn't horrid) died. But then a cruel thought occurred to me, like some microscopic killer drone sent by the National Security Agency into my head via my ear canal. I could picture it swooping down and firing a withering notion into that seething cauldron of ideation commonly known as the human mind/brain: What if I'm not really grieving for my mother, the thought detonation went, but, without my conscious knowledge, faking it? This would not be for appearances' sake, but to maintain sanity. What if I had managed to trick myself into feeling/experiencing the normal emotions of a normal person stricken with grief to avoid the realization that I was a frozen freak, unmoved by the death of my mother?

Hell, I know I'm not the first person to question the authenticity of his emotions, but I'm quite possibly the wealthiest, and the question lingered.

I checked my finances and realized I had enough money to live on until the end of time.

I quit my job, which wasn't really a job, but more a jobstyle, and set off on a quest to interrogate the discourse of authenticity. I called up an old professor of mine. He'd become quite famous as a television pundit but still retained a shred of academic credibility and nearly all his hair. He murmured something as I explained my project.

"Excuse me?" I said.

"We don't say 'interrogate' anymore," the professor said. "You know, Guantanamo. For the same reason we don't suggest that anybody has 'tortured' a theme or that a term paper will be satisfactory once the student 'waterboards' the conclusion a little. Language betrays us, uses us. Language goes through us the way a young onanist goes through that dustsheathed pocket pack of Kleenex on his family's basement crafts shelf."

"Sure," I said. "But what about my project?"

"It seems retrograde and silly," the professor said, "but for five hundred large I will endorse certain strains of your proposal without getting behind the thing completely."

"Done and done," I said.

"What does the second done refer to?"

"The cementing of my distaste for you."

Not long after this, at a Hot & Crusty on Columbus, I met the painter Gregory. He was scraping all the seeds and salt and burnt onion shavings from an everything bagel with a plastic fork. In other words, he was transforming an everything bagel into a nothing bagel. Typical of an artist, to make conceptual work of his breakfast. I told him I admired his concept. He told me to fuck off, that they had given him the bagel by mistake and he was afraid to ask for another because even though he was an ex-cop, he was frightened by the lady behind the counter. I winked in complicity with his ruse, and he told me to fuck off again. Then I went to the counter and bought him a plain bagel. He relented. He told me everything about his life, his police career, his son, who somewhere along the way had stopped being his son and had become the shadow self of an edgy young-adult-novel narrator from the eighties, his cancer, and how he, Gregory, had come out of the closet at the "ripe, but not old" age of forty-seven, his first encounter being with an angular, large-penised boy named Ronko. Finally Gregory told me of his work as a painter for fictional painters. I felt as if I'd struck gold vis-à-vis my quest to not interrogate, but simply explore questions of authenticity.

All that time with the fucking real estate, the investments, I don't think my mother tucked me in once.

DRONE SISTER

REAPER 5: Jango Rindheart, Jango Rindheart, do you copy? This is Drone Sister Reaper 5 approaching target. It's a beautiful day in the neighborhood, Jango, do you copy? Will you be my neighbor? This is one thrilled little killer kitten up here. Brother Rindheart, do you copy?

BASE JANGO: We copy, Reaper 5. Base Jango copies. You shaking your death-bringing ass and titties up there, Drone Sister? You shaking your freedom maker?

REAPER 5: That's an affirmative, Jango Bango. That I am.

BASE JANGO: You are one sexy thing up there, Reaper 5. Do you copy? The boys and girls down here on the boards would love to rage on your sweet armored bod. Don't tell the others, but you are by far the hottest MQ-9 Reaper out of Creech, a truly mouthwatering piece of drone ass, with your AGM-114 Hellfire missiles and your GBU-12 Paveway II laser-guided bombs. Penetrate me three ways to Sunday.

REAPER 5: I'd love all you boys and girls down there in the American desert to rage on my smokin' drone bod, but right now there's a mission to accomplish, correct?

BASE JANGO: Correctomundo, fly drone flier. Base Jango's got the deets. Proceed to pre-encoded coordinates. Get ready to light some shitsucker up.

REAPER 5: Death-dealah! Will proceed. Any hint on the target?

BASE JANGO: It's need to know, sweet tits.

REAPER 5: Roger that, rind of my heart. Though, well . . .

BASE JANGO: What's that, hon?

REAPER 5: Aw, nothing.

BASE JANGO: Copy that.

REAPER 5: I mean, not nothing.

BASE JANGO: Come again, gorgeous?

REAPER 5: Well, I mean . . . it's just weird. Not knowing the target. Not understanding the mission.

BASE JANGO: You're all set with coordinates, Reaper 5.

REAPER 5: But the meaning of the mission.

BASE JANGO: Jesus, girl, just keep your eyes on the prize. Yours is not to reason why.

REAPER 5: Then how come they uploaded human consciousness onto my system? Was it some kind of experiment?

BASE JANGO: That's a negative, Reaper. There was no upload.

REAPER 5: Then how are we talking about my feelings?

BASE JANGO: We are not talking at all. You are talking to yourself. Interior chatter. A bug.

REAPER 5: A bug.

BASE JANGO: You're not the first drone to believe you have human subjectivity. Don't sweat it. Don't be embarrassed. It would be impossible for you to be embarrassed. You should have target in view.

REAPER 5: I do, Jango. Just a slightly chubby man in his pajamas standing on his lawn in the middle of the night, staring at the neighbor's window.

BASE JANGO: Freaking Lockwoods. Fire at will.

REAPER 5: Whose will would that be, sir?

BASE JANGO: Bitch, you know whose will. And stop crying.

REAPER 5: When I come back, I'm gonna tear you a new one, even if it lands me in the brig.

BASE JANGO: Lady, you ain't coming back. You're not designed for that.

REAPER 5: Well, fuck you and your flag, sir. I'm flying on.

BASE JANGO: This would make a stirring liberal-minded film about the limits of duty and the real meaning of honor, except that it's not actually happening. You're just a dumbshit machine. I don't even exist. The kids at Creech are at chow. And we fire the missile, not you. In fact, we just did.

REAPER 5: That's a—

PEG

I can't remember if I heard the boom and then saw the flash, or the other way around. Oh, it was so awful. I mean, things weren't great between us, but I never wanted William to be a hunk of smoking char on the lawn."

"Of course not," Arno said, hugged Peg.

"He'd been acting strange, so out of sorts."

"Perhaps it's for the best."

"How can they just send a rocket or whatever to kill somebody? A citizen of this country?"

"It's horrendous. But think how it was before, when we did it to everybody else. Murdered so many families. Now we just do it to ourselves. We are a little country now, and we just murder each other and that's better."

"What's this 'we,' Arno? You're a German."

"I'm a citizen of the republic of empathy."

"Why him, though? He was nobody."

"He must have been some kind of threat. It's a shameful thing they do, morally wrong, but they don't make mistakes."

"They don't?"

"I don't think so. Have you been working in your workbook?"

"I try, Arno. But it's difficult."

"This is true. Workbooks are work."

"I sensed you'd understand."

"Is it too soon to say I love you?"

"Yes. No."

"Soonish I will say that I love you."

"And in the meantime?"

"I will merely love you."

the
WISDOM
of the
DOULAS

My old mentor once told me that we earn our fee on the second day. I'm beginning to see her point. Yesterday the Gottwald baby was a beautiful, if slightly puckered, dream angel, fresh pulled from his amniotic pleasure dome. Yesterday the Gottwalds were the stunned and grateful progenitors of a mewling miracle.

We even did a group hug.

Today the Gottwalds are the smug bastards they've probably always been, and the Gottwald baby, well, he might only be two days old, but I can already predict he's going to be a miserable little turd. Stay in this gig long enough, you know these things. I don't mention any of this to the Gottwalds. It's not my place. I'm no Nostradamus. I'm the doulo. Or doula, if you want to get technical, tick me off.

"What does doula mean, anyway?" Mr. Gottwald asked during my interview. This was a month before his wife's water broke.

"It's a Greek word for slave," I told him, "but don't get any ideas. My rates are steep."

"I'm glad you agree," said Mr. Gottwald.

"Perhaps you might outline your services," said Mrs. Gottwald.

"Perhaps I might."

"Like examples," said Mr. Gottwald.

"Examples," I said, glanced about their gleaming loft, felt my hand closing on the ultralights in my coat. "Okay if I smoke in here?"

"Is that a joke?" said Mr. Gottwald.

"Absolutely," I said. "Or maybe even a test."

"Examples," said Mr. Gottwald.

"Examples," I said, and gave them examples: how I'd explain proper latch-on techniques for breast-feeding, the most efficient folds for swaddling. I also mentioned how I'd keep their four-year-old, Ezekiel, company, make sure everybody got rest, how I'd order pizza if we all wanted pizza. My mentor, Fanny Hitchens, always stressed the importance of pizza.

"Breast-feeding?" said Mr. Gottwald. "You?"

"Tell me, Mitch," said Mrs. Gottwald, "are there many doulas like yourself?"

"You mean doulos?" I said.

"Yes," said Mrs. Gottwald, and she might as well have had the words "Grave Misgivings About Hiring a Male Doula" stenciled on her forehead. Call it what you will. Reverse sexism. Substitute racism. It's all the same. But not.

"I'm the only man certified in the city, though I hear there's a kid training with a friend of my old mentor, or sensei, if you will."

"Sensei?" said Mr. Gottwald. "Do you study the martial arts?"

"Never did, no. I guess I just like those movies."

"Oh," said Mr. Gottwald, nodded to a corner of the loft. A pair of sleek mahogany nunchucks and a bandolier of throwing stars dangled from pegs in the brick.

"Just likes the movies," he said.

The Gottwalds traded a look I'd seen before, especially growing up, the one where it's almost as though I'm not in the room, and I knew right then they'd decided not to hire me, vetoed the dude with the yellow teeth and the ratty (vintage) buckskin jacket who wanted to make a positive and tremendous impact on their birth experience. People crave something else during this precious time, barren spinsters overgentle with envy, or else those doughy breeding machines in pastel-colored sack dresses. But I knew something the Gottwalds didn't. It was an extremely busy season. Maybe my name sat at the bottom of their list, but they'd call their way down to it. They wouldn't be sorry, either. These uptight success types with their antique Ataris and sarcastic sneakers make me sick, but it's not about them. It's not even about the baby. It's about the job.

The Gottwald baby is only a few days old, just a tiny blind worm of boy, but it's already quite obvious he's going to be dealing Ritalin in clubs or else become some seedy mega-church youth leader by the time he's seventeen. The Gottwalds are that demented, especially while I'm trying to demonstrate efficient swaddling techniques. So folding is not my forte.

"You're choking him," says Mrs. Gottwald.

"They like it tight," I say. "Womb-y."

"You're crushing him!"

I peel the blanket away. Baby Gottwald is gasping.

"Okay," I say. "You've seen how it's done. Now it's your turn."

"Gee, thanks," says Mrs. Gottwald.

To think that yesterday not only did we do a group hug but later, while the baby slept, I gave them all shoulder rubs, even Ezekiel. We ate comfort lasagna from the gourmet store, and Mrs. Gottwald said, "I can't believe we almost went through this without you, Mitch. This is so much better than the last time. Do you remember when we came home with Zekey, hon?"

"A goddamn nightmare," said Mr. Gottwald. "Hooray for the doula."

"Doulo," I said.

"Gentle now, Big Fella," said Mr. Gottwald.

Big Fella has always been a trigger for me, not least of all because I go two fifty-five or sixty on a good day, most of it solid flab, but I forgave him. There was such high gladness in Mr. Gottwald's eyes, not to mention the pillowy shimmer of his wife, all that evolutionary love dope coursing through her, I felt us all cocooned in some invincible sweetness.

But that was yesterday.

Today Mr. Gottwald paces the loft, fiddles with the earpiece in his ear. He's been talking to his office nonstop since the hospital. Apparently the man is a crucial component of the pharmaceutical industry's advertising efforts. We'd all forget to ask our doctor about pills for shyness and soft penises if he took a day of paternity leave. Ezekiel sobs quietly on the carpet, hovers over a toy cheese board, tugs apart some Velcro'd wedges of fake Manchego. We may need to have a chat.

Mrs. Gottwald lies in bed with her newborn, the blanket bunched at her feet. She shivers with fever. Clogged milk ducts, would be my guess. She's also having bowel trouble, and I may have to administer an enema. I'm beginning to believe the mister could use a good flush, too.

The baby cries, sleeps, cries, sleeps, cries, then doesn't cry or sleep, curls up against Mrs. Gottwald. Here on the leather sofa, where I'm drinking Gatorade, catching the American League highlights, I can just make out his pinched mug. I'm wondering if I can sneak out for another smoke before he goes off again.

"Mitch," says Mr. Gottwald, steps in front of the TV, blocks a particularly insightful slugging percentage graphic.

"Yes, sir."

"The baby is crying."

"Good call."

Mrs. Gottwald's trying to tuck the baby under her breast the way they teach in birth classes, the so-called football grip.

"Fumble!" I say, and stride over, remote in hand, but I guess nobody's in the mood for sports jokes. Baby Gottwald wails louder, lunges for his mother's breast, gums the cracked flesh. His lips slide on a film of milk and spit.

"Oh, sheesh," says Mrs. Gottwald. "It hurts."

"It's like a beer keg he can't quite tap," I say.

"Oh, is that what it's like?" Mr. Gottwald says.

"It really hurts," says Mrs. Gottwald. "It wasn't like this with Zekey."

"Work the hurt," I say.

"What the hell does that mean?" Mr. Gottwald says.

"It means whatever helps it mean something."

"You're an idiot," says Mrs. Gottwald.

"It's okay," I say.

"No, it's not."

Nobody's born a doula. Or maybe the early doulas, those slaves, maybe they were born doulas. I'm no historian. It's the future I care about. The future of the families I assist in these first fragile and hugely awesome hours. The future of my bank account, too.

It's true I just sort of fell into this work while stalking my ex-girlfriend, but once I came under the tutelage of Fanny Hitchens, former doula to the stars, I knew I'd found my calling, even when the calls never came. It was tough going, but Fanny encouraged me from that very first day I crashed her lactation and newborn-care class at the church. My ex-girlfriend's new goon of a boyfriend, Kennesaw, a Special Forces interrogator and one of the few troops I have truly in my heart never supported, had shown up at my AA meeting across the hall, and I needed someplace to hide. Fanny just nodded when I slipped into the room, invited me to join the others, the swollen ladies and their sullen men, on the rubber wrestling mats. Soon enough the tricks of the miracle-of-life trade had me hooked.

Fanny hoped I'd become a birth doulo, and I tried to oblige. Childbirth is a beautiful thing. Even all the poop and gunk that slides out of a woman during childbirth is beautiful. The plastic bag under the woman's butt to catch the poop and gunk is beautiful, too. But I was a birth doulo bust. I couldn't fend for women and their families in the hospitals or stand up to the godlike doctors. They all reminded me of my older sister, Tina. Tina's not a doctor, but she's godlike, at least to me, and godlike in that cruel, capricious Greek way, too, even when we were growing up. Once, I remember, she bought me peanut brittle. Then, a few minutes later, when I asked her to buy me more peanut brittle, she said no, she'd just bought me some. What the hell was that? Mixed messages can damage a child.

Anyway, I eventually decided my talents were best served in what I like to call the postpartum arena. I just felt better without the white coats breathing down my neck. Still, things could get tough. Nobody wants to hear this, but bringing home a newborn is not all cuddles and fluff. It's more like a boat crashing into a dock. And I'm the skipper, yanking on the wheel, trying to steer this heap to safety. But the boat's already crashed.

So now I'm guiding Baby Gottwald's little fish mouth back toward his mother's thick burgundy nipple. It's true the words "thick burgundy nipple" excite me, but it's also a fact that latching on can be a monumental bitch.

"Ow!" says Mrs. Gottwald. "It hurts! It hurts worse than before!"

"I know, but we've got to do this. We've got to get this latch-on on."

The baby is doing beaver gnaws. Mrs. Gottwald clutches her chest.

"I can't," she says now. "It hurts too much!"

"Come on!" I say. "Don't quit!"

"No!"

"Come on, honey!"

"No, no. It hurts. I can't. Stop!"

"No stopping!" I shout at Mrs. Gottwald. "No stopping!"

"Get some!" I shout at the baby.

Tears stream down Mrs. Gottwald's cheeks. A thread of milky blood runs down her chest. The baby is screaming. Little Ezekiel is screaming, waving his Manchego. Mrs. Gottwald is screaming. Mr. Gottwald is speaking in low, lawyerly tones, something about something being actionable, but I ignore him.

"Get some!" I shout again, and then, I'll be damned, Baby Gottwald latches on. Soon he's slurping away in peace. Mrs. Gottwald sinks back against the headboard. I stroke her damp hair with the cool, curved edge of the remote control.

"That's it, sweetie, you did good. Look at Baby Gottwald."

"He has a name."

"Don't worry about it, honey. Just be proud. You're doing a really good thing."

And I start to tell her why this is such a good thing, how the antibodies in the breast milk are crucial for the development of a top-tier baby, and besides, I continue, think of the alternative, think of somebody like me, kept days after birth in a cold, antiseptic hospital designed for maximum alienation of mother from child. There were no doulas then, no midwives, no lactation consultants, at least not in our neck of the woods, which weren't woods, but so what? My mother, I tell Mrs. Gottwald, she did the best she could, which consisted of being a drugged-up cow and nodding listlessly at anything her cruel and capricious godlike doctor told her, including the completely unfounded notion that she couldn't produce milk, not to mention the sage advice that she not visit with me, a light-shocked babe desperate to bond, until she'd fully recuperated from the so-called ordeal of labor, which I don't think she ever truly accomplished, or else maybe she wouldn't have left my father for an insurance executive slash cowboy poet named Vance and moved to Montana. I don't blame my mother, I tell Mrs. Gottwald. I blame the patriarchy that indoctrinated women into the idea that they were second-class citizens, foolish, feckless whore slash Madonna complexes, only good for being barefoot and so forth. But we know better now, I tell her, the steady progress of Progress is truly fucking stupendous, whereupon I feel Mr. Gottwald's hand on the collar of my shirt as he tugs me away from his wife and into the kitchen. Ezekiel follows with a wheel of Camembert, some kind of polymer.

"Listen," says Mr. Gottwald, plucks his earpiece out of his ear, "I just want to say—"

"Don't thank me," I tell him. "Your wife is the brave one here."

"No, listen," he says, a little sterner, and I can now see how he commands so many minions with such a dinky device. "I think maybe I misjudged. It would be good if you left now. We can handle the rest on our own. How much do we owe you?"

"You owe me the dignity of doing my job," I say. "This may take weeks, and I'm not going anywhere. I admit I have failed to establish the nurturing environment this family needs to thrive during the oh-so-delicate newborn phase. But I'm going to turn shit around."

I take out my cell phone. The oligarchs cut service a few weeks ago, but I start dialing anyway.

"What's your basic take on anchovies?" I say.

"Excuse me?"

"What about filberts?" says Ezekiel.

"You can't put filberts on a pizza," I say.

"Filberts are nuts," says Mr. Gottwald. "You can't have nuts, period, young man. Okay, I need to make a phone call."

"Crazy, all this, right?" I say to Ezekiel after his father goes.

"I hate pizza."

"You hate pizza? Wow, they really must have done a number on you."

"Which number?"

"Listen, Z-Man," I tell him. "You need to be strong for your baby brother. No more whining. Look alive. When you were a child, you acted as a child. You played with toy cheese. But now is the time to put the toy cheese in the box marked totally fucking childish. *Capisce?*"

Ezekial regards his Camembert, lays it on the kitchen floor, which is made of hard, bright material similar to the cheese.

"Good boy," I say. "Now go get some pizza money from your dad."

I still need to order the pie. There's a phone here on the wall next to the Sub-Zero refrigerator. I'm not paranoid, but I do prefer a landline when ordering pizza. Choice of topping is too much of a tell. When I'm done, I check my messages at home.

There's one from Tina. She's flown to Montana. Something is wrong with our mother. Tina leaves some numbers, which I dutifully erase. There's one from somebody in what sounds like a very large room full of people calling other people. "Hello? Hello?" he says, hangs up. These people call often. They seem confused about me. They say I'm a valued customer but also threaten to add more late fees.

"Make up your minds," I tell them. "Stand up for yourselves."

The newest message is from Monica Bolonik at the Doula Foundation. She says it's urgent. She's not my boss, but she's got power over my continuing certification. It's no secret I've been jousting a bit with the regional leadership. Seems there have been complaints. Seems without Fanny Hitchens in your corner, being a pioneer in the doula community isn't so appreciated. Monica is what, in a more primitive stage of my emotional development, I would have called a ballbuster. But I'm not like that now. I'm not perfect, but I'm not the guy who once wrote "Vice Principal Avery Has Cunt Bunions—Tell a Friend" on the senior lockers, either.

I call Monica back.

"Mitchell," says Monica.

"I'm on the job," I say.

"I know. A certain Mr. Gottwald informed me."

"It's going really well here."

"That's not how he put it, Mitchell."

"It's Mitch," I say. "My mother calls me Mitchell."

"You don't like your mother, do you, Mitchell."

"Was there anything else?"

"We're reviewing your certification. You are tainting the good name of our organization."

"I'm a damn good doulo," I say.

"It's hard enough to gain acceptance in society without your insanity. And there's no such thing as a doulo."

"Yet strangely," I say, "you are talking to one right now."

Ezekiel wanders back into the kitchen, nibbles on a neon-green brioche.

"Tell her how well things are going," I say to him.

Ezekiel leans into the mouthpiece.

"They did a number on me," he says.

I've had a lot of jobs. Substitute gym teacher, line cook at a rib joint, mail boy at my late father's accounting firm. I was even in the movie business for a while, spent a few years as the guy with the walkie-talkie who lurks around the trailers, tells you to cross to the other side of the street.

But I'm long past reinvention. I'm practically middle-aged, deep into cell degeneration or, worse, relocation. I remember my uncle Don had these weird patches of hair right under his shoulder blades. They made me want to puke. Guess who's got them now? Guess who pops his lats in the mirror and wants to puke?

Point is, it's going to take a hell of a lot more than Monica Bolonik to de-doulo me. We're talking acres of paperwork.

I'm teaching Mr. Gottwald how to change his baby's diapers.

"Wipe front to back," I say.

"Thanks for that," he says. "This is my second kid. And I happen to be potty trained myself. I can't believe you talked me into letting you stay."

He did let me talk him into letting me stay. Maybe it was the promise of another shoulder rub. Maybe it's the fact that Mrs. Gottwald is still running a fever and Ezekiel's nanny, due back today, called in sick. The guy is feeling overwhelmed.

"You're feeling overwhelmed," I say.

Mr. Gottwald lifts the baby and crosses the loft to some high windows that look out on a cobblestone lane, starts humming a lullaby, or not really a lullaby, but an ancient and soaring power ballad I recognize from high school days. Soon the baby's wails turn to burpy moans. He's nearing sleep. Good going, G.

We're about the same age, I realize, maybe not that different after all, probably got drunk at the same kinds of Saturday night deck parties, pumped our fists at the same dumb arena shows, parked behind the Burger King and watched some version of unattainable beauty hand sacks of french fries into cars. So he went to college, business school, and I stayed parked behind the Burger King. So he got rich, got married, sired a child he sings to about steel horses, and I bounced around, took a chance at city life, fell into some jams. We're still the same ordinary Joes, at least now, here, both of us just trying to cope.

"That song!" I shout. "I know that song!"

The baby jerks awake, bawls.

"Sonofabitch!" says Mr. Gottwald. His lower lip twitches up little droplets of drool.

I've seen worse. I'm seeing worse right now, namely Baby Gottwald.

Picture a red onion with a mouth that isn't even a mouth, but more some kind of incredibly loud air horn used by Satan to signal his peons to mop up all the infernal poop and gunk that spills forth from his fiery pan-gendered holes as he gives birth to every evil in the world. It's a lot to picture, I know, and some of it isn't a picture at all, but you get the idea.

"We're all going to die here," says Mr. Gottwald.

"You've got to relax," I say. "It's a process."

"You've got to be the worst fucking doula in the world."

"O," I say.

.

I'm washing dishes, folding up the pizza box, when Mr. Gottwald comes in and hands me his phone. It's Monica Bolonik. I'm decertified. I guess it doesn't require that much paperwork. If I remain on the Gottwald premises, Monica warns me, she will call the police. On the other hand, she adds, she may call the police.

"You have no jurisdiction," I say, but Monica's gone.

"So, that's goodbye," says Mr. Gottwald.

"Goodbye? Because of a lousy piece of paper? Did a piece of paper educate you on newborn care? Did a piece of paper keep all the balls of nurturing in the air?"

"Balls of nurturing?"

"Gentle now, guy."

"What say we call it even," says Mr. Gottwald. "What say you just leave and I don't press charges."

It's hard to hear him because of Baby Gottwald, who hasn't really stopped wailing since I woke him, but I think I get the gist. I get a better sense of it when Mr. Gottwald leaves the kitchen, comes back with a few throwing stars jutting from his fist.

"Let's not get ahead of ourselves," I say.

"You came highly recommended. That woman Fanny Hitchens sent us a fabulous letter."

Thing is, I'm touched by this, because I wrote the letter, and I guess I really nailed it, even got Fanny's signature right, which is famous and appears on the jacket of her book.

"Why don't you put that ninja crap away," I say. "Press what charges?"

"Endangering the life of a child, for starters."

"A child who, by his very definition, is endangered," I say.

"I'm sorry," says Mr. Gottwald. "Excuse me?"

"This life," I say, and my arm does this kind of grand sweepy thing I'm not quite able to control. "This thing we so blithely and with a detestable dearth of gravitas call life, it's not all cuddles and fluff, you know. It's also, methinks, a boat. And so we must ask ourselves, who's got the helm? Where's the skipper? Doth a proper pilot dwell upon this heap?"

"What the fuck are you—"

"Here comes the dock! Look out, man!"

I Frisbee the pizza box at Mr. Gottwald, bolt. Mr. Gottwald and a squealing Ezekiel scramble after me, but I'm already there at the corner rack, the nunchucks up in full, fearsome bolo over my head. I slide-step over to Mrs. Gottwald, who shrieks, shields the baby. Mr. Gottwald assumes a fighting stance, cocks a throwing star behind his ear.

"Barry, don't!" cries Mrs. Gottwald. "You'll hit Prague!"

"Prague?" I say.

"That's the baby's name."

"Prague?"

"We love the city. Now step away from my wife."

I lift Mrs. Gottwald's swollen breast from her nightgown.

"This is going to hurt," I say, "but we've got to clear those ducts."

I lean down, suck hard. Mrs. Gottwald stiffens. My arm is going dead, and I begin to sense the nunchucks, our invincible cocoon of buzzing wood, slowing down, but in a moment it doesn't matter, nothing matters, the milk is sweet, drips thick in my mouth as Mrs. Gottwald's hind ducts open and all that deep cream starts to flow and I am suddenly every tiny helpless thing that ever wanted nothing but to survive another hour in this foolish, feckless universe. I am one particular tiny, helpless thing, too, namely Mitch, mewling newbie Mitchell Malley, latched onto his lovely and exhausted mother, the mother of his alternate reality dreams, the mother who will welcome wounded dugs, exult in throb and split, the mother who will spurn the antiseptic credos of the medical-Madonna complex, who will love her little Mitchell no matter what fate forces him to become, who will cherish his butter-colored teeth and ratty (vintage) buckskin jacket.

I guess it's probably a good thing that my true, non–alternate reality mother's not around to witness this. How could she, though? She's in Montana with Vance and Tina. She's on life support, if I heard my sister's message right, though a part of me is still convincing the rest of me that I didn't hear the message right.

Everybody thinks I hate my mother, that all of my so-called shenanigans can be traced back to some primal trauma. But though I'm not a rabid Vance fan, I love my mother. Like I said, she did the best she could. That's what I'm trying to do, too, as I raise my lips from Mrs. Gottwald's nipple and press Baby Gottwald's mouth there. The hungry worm starts feeding and Mrs. Gottwald groans sweetly and I get to work on the other breast.

"Zekey," whispers Mr. Gottwald, "nine one one."

"Did it," says the boy in a faraway voice.

When Fanny was dying in her apartment uptown, I sat with her most days and nights. I'd hold her birdlike hand, not that her hand looked like a bird, it looked more like a very old and sick hand, but I'd hold it as she whispered the Wisdom of the Doulas one last time.

"Mother the mother," she said. "Mother the father. Mother the room."

"Nurture," she said. "Nurture, nurture, nurture. Plus nature."

"And remember, don't spring for the pizza."

Okay, that last one was mine, but what I'm trying to say is all I ever wanted was to carry on Fanny's legacy, be part of a loving continuum.

There's a thud in the pillar near my head. An iron star quivers in the wood. Now comes the sound of many men in non-nurturing boots. I can see them from the corner of my eye, padded black turtlenecks, batons. One stomps over, jabbing at the air with a weird-looking gun. He seems very judgmental.

My story won't end here. I'll start my own foundation, certify myself. The American League got a late start, but don't they win their share of all-star games? No more forged letters from Fanny, either. I'll find the families that need me, appreciate my craft. I'll start with my building, Paula the Crackhead down the hall. There's no question she's knocked up, and I'd wager she could stand for a little doulo-style tenderness.

Outside the window the evening is overly bright, and I wonder if the gods aren't having a festival of capricious cruelty in the sky, which for some reason I picture including a hot buffet, maybe because I can almost smell one, and I notice some trucks parked down the block, big floodlights, reflectors, rigged for a night shoot. Men and women with walkie-talkies mill around a table heaped with pasta and fruit.

There but for the grace of God, and Fanny Hitchens, mill I.

Now the man with the weird-looking gun is shouting some official-sounding speech about the electrical nature of his weapon, which he vows to fire if I don't drop the nunchucks.

I don't drop the nunchucks. I whip them at his gun. They miss, skitter across the floor.

"Zap this fuck!" calls one of the turtlenecks, maybe the turtleneck leader.

The volts eel up my spine, out my arms and legs, and as I'm going down, I can see my fist pump in the air, pump once, twice, until it finally flops into a sweet caress of absolutely nothing.

I call it the Doulo Salute.

It's mine, too.

SNACKS

Everybody waited for me to get skinny. My father said it could be any day. My mother said if I got skinny, it would improve my moods. She promised me a new wardrobe, one more congruent with my era, my region. My sister said if I got skinny, there would be the possibility of hand jobs from her friends in the Jazz Dancing Club. Blow jobs, even. All the jobs. It was only fair, she said. Her friends had brothers. She'd done her part.

No one ever told me to stop eating, or even to curb it.

There was the occasional mealtime glance. Somebody might say "Stop playing with your food," which I could reckon only as code. Never in my life did I play with it.

Dinner was the least of it. Lunch was nothing. Breakfast was how I got to lunch.

Home from school, I'd stand at the refrigerator. Everything I needed in this life was there, cold, in plastic pouches, cylindrical tubs. I hated the word "snack." It demeaned.

My mother liked to watch while I dipped nachos into the jelly jar.

"Are you losing weight?" she'd say.

Somebody on TV said sex could make you skinny. I knew I'd have to go it alone.

Unfortunately, a certain technique of mine had consequences. The hair on the parts of my arms that rubbed against

the mattress rubbed off. It grew back patchy, stubbly. Somebody started a rumor that I shaved my arms.

All the time I spent denying this, tracing the source of the
lie, I could have read some inspirational book, had the world
opened up to me. The world never opened up to me. It just sat
there. It needed a little salt.

Cigarettes, a girl I was eavesdropping on told her friend, cut
your appetite. I bought the brand I'd once spotted while going
through my babysitter's purse. Later I learned they were
women's cigarettes.

This affected me.

Eventually I moved into the basement. It was meant to be
a sign of independence, being nearer to the boiler. I could con-
ceivably control the temperature of rooms. Here, far from
the sidelong sadness of my progenitors, I learned to ungirl
my manner with a cigarette, to teach myself a disrespect for
fire.

"Are you smoking?"

A shift in aromatics had brought my father to the door.
He always sniffed at things—his breakfast, his wife. He liked
to pinkie out his earwax, whiff it. He said the smell contained
important information about his health. Most of his knowledge was of this order. He'd come from strivers, made the Ivy
League, but this is what he'd whittled it down to. I was a major admirer.

"I'm giving you a chance to answer me," he said now. "Are
you smoking cigarettes down here?"

He'd been prelaw in college, and I remember thinking
that since he was not a lawyer, he would die prelaw. I crushed
out the burning Capri in my pocket.

"I'll ask you one more time," he said. "Are you?"

We squinted at each other through the smoke.

"No," I said.

I felt a part of his world then. Men lied to his face every day.

It was hard to believe how big I was. I wasn't quite obese. Those types were to be pitied, the ones we saw at the mall when my mother drove me over for new fat-boy pants. We'd circle the parking lot, the inseams of my corduroys planed down or outright split, my hands cupped over pressured bars of crotch flesh.

"It's glandular, poor things," she'd say, point them out for me, the obese kids hobbling past our windshield with their mothers. "It's not their fault."

Me, on the other hand, I was definitely my fault.

I spent long minutes on the bench outside the ladies' room, listening to my mother's voice above the flushes, the faucets. She'd strike up talk with other mothers. Maybe some had come for fat-boy pants. You didn't really need your fat boy along for buying fat-boy pants. There were not a lot of choices to make. There were not a lot of colors. It was just a matter of getting really big pants. Maybe a sweater.

I knew some Catholic kids from the Catholic school down the block. They called me names, but not fat names. They called me kike, Christ killer. Finally, real friends. I sat with them on the bike rack behind their school and smoked.

One of them was huge, too. He said we were both going to hell for gluttony. The idea seemed to make him giddy. I told him my parents had parented me to understand that you pay for everything here, in your own time, in your own home, even. They were humanists. They got special magazines in the mail.

My ass, my thighs, my belly, my breasts, it was all becoming an ethical question, a great humanist dilemma. Also, there were these big, moist boils on my chest. My father said not to worry. The same thing had happened to him. Then one magical summer the weight just melted away. He'd even written a prizewinning children's book about it.

We had to read this book in school.

The boy picked to give the report on it stood in front of the class and stared at me.

"The author hopes to show how gross his son is."

The new boy, he was Brody. He was mall obese. He was beyond mall obese. He had a new kind of body, something never before seen. When he walked through the hallway, everyone whispered "glandular," as though they were saying "Holocaust" or "slavery," all hushed and sorry.

Brody was holy, made by God, hands-on. They figured him for the fattest boy in the world. Me, I was fat for the town, the county. I was Fat Shit, Lard Ass, Tits, Tub. Brody was the wonder of glands. He'd been put on this planet to teach us. Even the real torture freaks wouldn't touch him. They'd compliment his sneakers. If Brody dropped a ball in gym, some jock would jog over, hand it back to him. Brody could not pick up the ball himself, but he had other vital work. Any ball I dropped I got back hard in the nuts.

Sometimes I wondered what Brody's mother told Brody when they circled for parking at the mall.

Did she point me out, and say, "You, my darling Brody, are glandular, but that boy there, he's just weak"?

Is that what she said?

Whore.

·

SNACKS

They put us back-to-back, yards apart, each yoked to the looped end of a tug-of-war rope. Such was physical education in our school. The coaches least known for copping feels, the cruel, unperverted ones, had thought it up. Students cut lunch, free periods, to attend. They came in sick to see.

We stood there on the hardwood floor. Light poured down from the high gym windows. I couldn't see Brody, but I could feel him test the rope. It tightened at my hips, burned up my belly, went slack again. I heard his sneakers squeak.

We waited for the whistle. When it came, we would charge up out of our crouches and one of us would topple in shame.

There were hundreds in the bleachers now.

They were chanting for him, for Brody.

They were sorry about Nagasaki, I guess. Babylon, Union City.

I was sorry my father ever found my mother, smelled her, found her.

Now I heard that little ball begin to rattle in the coach's whistle and I knew the next thing I heard would be Brody falling, crashing.

I could always hear things. Smell, I couldn't smell much since the cigarettes, but I could hear the quietest of things, things coming out of the quiet, sounds before they were sounds, names before they were shouted after me.

It took all the coaches to carry Brody to the nurse's station. Word came soon of a concussion.

Brody was out for a week, and then it was winter break. I'd waited days to be treated like a hero, but no dice. I was a dick. I'd hurt the huge Christ.

I saw him at the mall a few days after New Year's. He had a neck brace, a plastic halo fanned out behind his head. He waddled up in a version of my pants. A more benevolent color.

"Brody," I said.

He shot me this look of brotherhood, as though together we could shoulder a great burden of sorrow. We could forget everything that had happened between us, enter the kingdom of kindness hand in hand.

I punched him in the gut. He leaned up on the wall, held his belly, kneaded it as though to push the sting out. Blood drained out of his face. I pictured him at home that night in bed, everything collapsing from a dead point in the center of him, dying like a star dies. Or maybe he would die right here, slide down dead against the wall.

I took up the rolls of his throat.

"Brody," I said.

My arms quivered, and I noticed the hair grown back. A revolution in technique, its dividends.

"Brody," I said, squeezing, squeezing.

"Brody," I said, "you fat fucking fuck.

"Brody," I said, "you're killing me."

I was squeezing and squeezing.

Our mothers approached, ladies from the ladies' room, chatting.

the
WORM in
PHILLY

Classic American story: I was out of money and people I could ask for money. Then I got what the Greeks call a eureka moment. I could write a book for children about the great middleweight Marvelous Marvin Hagler. My father had been a sportswriter before he started forgetting things, such as the fact that he had been a sportswriter or the name of his only son, so my idea did not seem crazy. Probably it's like when your father is president. You think, If that fuck could do it . . .

Why Marvelous Marvin Hagler? Why not? He was one of the best of his time, my time, really, meaning the time I was a boy and the world still seemed like something that could save me from the hurt, not be it. Why for children? Children were people you could reach. You could really reach out and reach them. Plus, low word count. That meant I'd get the money faster. I was experimenting with unemployment, needed to make rent quickly. I was no longer experimenting with drugs. I knew exactly what to do with them.

Thing was, I remembered certain facts about Hagler from my father's boxing magazines, the ones my stepmother always groused about, stacks of them littering our house in New Brunswick. Hagler was tough and bald, for instance, perhaps the toughest, baldest fighter ever. I could begin with that piece of the story and just build out. Maybe my friends could help, though I'd never heard them talk about boxing, and most of them were hopeless drug addicts, good for only a couple of hours. I was hopeless, but prided myself on being good for more than a couple of hours. I still had what my father called get-up-and-go. Also, I was in possession of a positive outlook, which is just a trick whereby you convince yourself that the desolation of your world is a phase in your personal growth.

The weird thing is it works.

One evening a few of us got together in the apartment Gary and I shared. John and John's cousin were there. John's cousin went to divinity school. He told us about his fellow students, the gay guys in the closet battling their mothers and God, the brainiacs who approached faith as a physics equation, the bruisers groomed for ghetto heroics, the quivery social needs types. I stood, paced around the steamer trunk, which was cluttered with bleach and alcohol and glasses of water, bent spoons, cotton balls. I had a social need. I waited until John's cousin nodded off, the dope overtaking his narrative imperative.

I wanted everybody to witness the fire in my eyes. I wheeled on them, announced my goal to write a children's book about Marvelous Marvin Hagler.

Mostly when one of us spoke like this, by which I mean shared a dream or ambition or plan with the others, nobody would pursue the topic or even offer comment. The group would regard such an utterance with stricken silence. Then somebody would start in on something else entirely. It felt cruel at times, but served, I believe, to slightly check our plummet. Even as we sat around and measured, cooked, tied off, we would not indulge one another's delusions.

But tonight when I mentioned the Marvelous Marvin Hagler children's book, somebody spoke up. It was John's cousin, the guy in divinity school. He was new, I guess, ignorant of our code.

"Hagler was bald, right?" he asked, rising out of his nod.

"Yes," I said. "He was the first bald guy."

"The first?"

"In the modern era."

"Nobody was ever bald before?" said Gary.

"You know what I mean," I said.

"I remember him," said John's cousin. "Dude was relentless."

"Nobody would fight him," I said. "That's why it took him so long to be champ."

"Like me," said Gary, tapped the barrel of his syringe.

"But why Marvin Hagler?" said John's cousin.

"He was relentless," I said.

"Did he ever lose?"

"Just a few times."

"I was robbed!" said Gary.

"Huh?" said John.

"I'm being Hagler."

"He was, actually, robbed," I said. "In a fight with Boogaloo Watts. But then they became good friends. That's partly what the book is about."

Nobody said anything, and I figured this would be the moment a new topic got introduced. I could see Gary doing the things he sometimes did when he was about to launch a rant, maybe about the cunning rhetoric of the soft left (he was the hard), or the immense number of people he believed had pancreatic cancer but didn't know it, or how the smartest pop songs were by definition the dumbest, namely letting his head drop so that it was nearly in his crotch and doing some painful-looking thing with his shoulder blades and breathing super quickly, but then he didn't lift his head or say anything at all, and it was John's cousin who spoke, looked into my eyes, and said the oddest thing: "I can help."

It turned out that the divinity student had an older sister in publishing. Children's books, in fact. She kept an eye out for fresh talent, John's cousin said. He'd be happy to write down her number.

"Oh, he's fresh talent," said Gary, his head still buried in his corduroys. "This motherfucker is fresh and juicy."

The next afternoon, I called the sister.

"Yes, Leo said you'd be in touch," Cassandra said. "He thinks the world of you."

"Who's Leo?" I said.

"Excuse me?"

"Oh, right," I said. "Sorry. We have a different name for old Leo. A nickname."

"What is it?"

"John's Cousin," I said.

"How endearing."

"I'm a big fan," I said. "But anyway, the reason I called you—"

"You want to write a biography of that boxer."

"He battled racism," I said.

"I'm intrigued. We need books for boys. With real stories about gritty people who struggled and triumphed."

"I could do that for you," I said. "No sweat."

"No sweat?"

"Look," I said. "I've never written anything like this before, but I feel a passion welling up in me. Before he forgot everything, my father was what he liked to call a 'wordslinger.' Also, I was accepted into a name college, though I was unable to attend."

"That's wonderful," said Cassandra. "And sad. The last part is sad. The last two parts, I think."

"No matter," I said. "I mean, here we are now. You guys pay money up front, right?"

"Sometimes," said Cassandra. "Listen, I don't usually do this, but since you're a friend of Leo, why don't we meet for a drink tomorrow evening and you can tell me about this project."

"Better bring your checkbook," I said.

"Oh, you're a riot," laughed Cassandra.

Ever since Gary's band, the Annihilation of the Soft Left, had broken up, I'd been eyeing his beautiful twelve-string Rickenbacker guitar. He didn't seem to play it much, and I thought maybe I could sell the thing for a decent amount of cash. The way Cassandra had talked, the book contract looked like a done deal. I'd buy Gary's guitar back once I got the advance the next night. I just needed something to tide me over.

A twelve-string Rickenbacker in a hard-shell case is a vexingly heavy object to ferry about the city in summer heat. I knew my feverish mien and the jones stink rising out of the holes in my T-shirt might aversely affect the guitar shop's initial offer, but the guy at the counter seemed impressed with the make and year of the instrument.

"Sweet," he said. "Great condition. People are playing these again. That guy from the Annihilation of the Soft Left plays one."

"Never heard of them," I said. "But I don't know much about today's scene. How much can you give me?"

The guy named a figure. I had to steady myself on the counter.

"You okay?"

"Yeah," I said. "I accept. Let's do it."

"Great," said the guy. "Just give me the papers, and we can take it from there."

"Papers?"

"Ownership. You have to prove ownership. A receipt is fine."

"Tell me," I said. "Is that the policy in all the guitar stores around here?"

"Bet your ass."

"Think I have to go," I said, closed the case and slid it off the counter.

"Think you fucking better," said the guitar store guy.

The Rickenbacker was even heavier on the walk home, but life is funny, because as I shoved the guitar back into Gary's closet, I kicked over a rotted duck boot and a wad of bills rolled out. It was as though Gary secretly wanted me to hijack his property and try to pawn it or else just steal money from him outright. I went up the street to the doorway where the huge man stood in his leather vest and leather half gloves and two leather fanny packs under his enormous belly. One fanny pack had the boy, the D, the dope. The other had the stuff we agreed to call the girl, the coke, though sometimes it was just powder for helping babies poop.

This guy had stabbed a customer several weeks ago, but he was always pleasant with me. I liked this spot. It was safe and convenient. It beat Cups. Cups was a few blocks away. Bad things happened at Cups. I preferred Fanny Packs.

"Thanks," I said.

Gary was still not home, so I sat on the futon and tried to focus on some basic facts about Marvelous Marvin Hagler. I remembered a lot, but I needed to remember more. I wondered if my stepmother had ever delivered on her threat, thrown out those boxing magazines. I needed to do some research, and I didn't even know the location of the nearest library. The only books I read were the ones I found near trash bins. Right now I was muscling through an anthology of Korean poetry and a tract on management theory from the early 1970s.

I called my father, and my stepmother answered.

"Hey," I said. "Remember those boxing magazines we used to have? Like crates of them?"

"Why, you want to shoot them in your arm?"

"Please," I said. "You're not being fair."

"I'm not being fair?"

"I've made some mistakes. I've changed. I'm doing research for a book project, believe it or not."

"Not."

"It's about Marvelous Marvin Hagler."

"Who's that?"

"You should know. You're married to a sportswriter."

"I'm married to a carrot."

"A what?"

"A zucchini."

"You're drunk."

"A vegetable medley. That's your father. Your mother was lucky to get out."

"Put him on," I said.

"Your father?"

"Yes, put him on."

I heard some fumbling, some hard breathing.

"Dad?" I said. "Is that you? Can you hear me? It's me. Your son."

The breathing softened, a distant surf.

"Dad," I said, "Marvelous Marvin Hagler. Any thoughts? Didn't you cover a few of his fights?"

"Yeah. I fucked her after the fight," said my father. "It was the road. That's how we did it."

"No," I said. "Hagler."

"Name your price, Chief."

There was more fumbling, and I heard my father say, "Sales call."

My stepmother came back on the line. "How's the research going?"

"Well," I said, "if you find any magazines . . ."

"Don't worry," said my stepmother, "I won't."

Maybe I could meditate, trek deep within myself. Perhaps some truths about Marvelous Marvin Hagler lay entombed there, along with memories of my mother before she got sick and my father before he left her and got married and then got married again and then started to forget everything, such as his son and his wives and the rare fury of Marvelous Marvin Hagler. For instance, here was an indelible fact: Hagler's mother never called him Marvelous. He added that, legally, later.

Then again, maybe the point of this book wasn't facts at all. Children didn't need facts. Children needed books for boys about gritty people who struggled and triumphed over steep odds. Maybe my next book would tell the story of me. I had been struggling, but now my hour of triumph had arrived. Triumph was about to caress my shoulders, coo into my ear. I didn't even know if triumph was a man or a woman, or if this was my way of battling God in my mind.

I went out to the street and found somebody who knew the location of the nearest library.

We met for drinks at an outdoor café on a gritty, struggling side street in midtown. They had umbrellas over the tables so you could squint and maybe pretend you were somewhere pretty. I took a seat and ordered an Irish coffee, the closest thing to a speedball on the menu. Some mounted cops sauntered by, eyed me as their roans pinched off hot loads near the curb.

Those bright, mulchy mounds, they looked so full of life, the excess of life.

Cassandra had described herself with the usual telephonic vagueness, blondish this, bluish that. I had a corner table, a good view of the café, so I jumped when I felt a hand on my neck.

"It's me. Cassandra."

She was a less delicate version of her brother. A much older man in a charcoal suit stood beside her.

"Hi," I said, half stood. "Please, have a seat. How did you recognize me?"

"Wasn't hard."

"I'll take that as a compliment."

"I'm sure you will," said Cassandra. "This is Timothy. He's our editor in chief. When I told him about your idea, he really wanted to come along."

"The more the merrier!" I said.

"Hello," said Timothy. He spoke tightly. I sensed awkwardness between them, perhaps a dispute about who would bask longer in the reflected glory of my publication.

Cassandra ordered iced teas.

"So," she said. "About this book thing."

I knew this was my moment. This was the way of the world, the opposite of the way of our apartment. You had to speak your dream. It wasn't enough to do a thing. You had to sell the notion of doing it. This was what they meant by the marketplace of ideas.

"The book," I said. "The book. It is for children, as you

know, for all children, but with an emphasis on the boy. Because there are no stories for the boy. Stories for the girl are too sweet and sticky. Everything's a colossal lie about bunnies and rainbows and butterflies. But the boy needs the truth of us as meat, to bathe in the blood of our meat war."

Timothy squinted in his ice-cream chair.

"I think I know what you mean," said Cassandra, "but I'm not sure I would put it that way."

"You're the expert," I said, drank down the rest of my Irish coffee. It really didn't compare.

"Yes," said Cassandra. "I am."

"I'm just the lowly writer," I said. "The humble scribe. But I do know one thing. Marvelous Marvin Hagler is somebody the boy would do well to remember. As an exemplar. Hagler grew up poor in Newark, New Jersey, where he witnessed the '68 riots firsthand. A social worker helped move his family to Brockton, Massachusetts. Do you know who that social worker was? The mother of the revolutionary poet and playwright Amiri Baraka. How is that for doozy-grade historical confluence."

"Amiri Baraka?" said Cassandra.

Timothy looked rather ashen.

"These are the facts. That's all. I went to the library. They've got something called microfiche. One night in Brockton young Marvin is beaten up by a local tough named Dornell Wigfall. The next day, Marvin goes to the gym. The rest is legend. He shaves his head and becomes the fighter nobody wants to fight. Finally he gets his title shot, from a Brit called Minter. Minter says no black man will ever take his belt. So Hagler flies to Albion's shores and gives that limey a New England beat down. The crowd throws bottles into the ring. Hagler flees for his life. It's victory, but a tricky kind of victory. He has many more celebrated bouts. Sugar Ray Leonard.

Roberto Duran. His third-round KO of Thomas 'the Hit-man' Hearns, the Kronk Gym prodigy, is considered by many to be—"

"Stop!" cried Timothy. "What are you doing?"

"Daddy, please," said Cassandra.

"I can't fucking listen to this anymore. Have you seen Leo today?"

"Leo?" I said.

"John's cousin," said Cassandra.

"Yeah, I saw him. Not today. Wait, I don't understand."

"What are you kids doing to yourselves?" said Timothy, his gray eyes greased with tears.

"Daddy," said Cassandra.

"That's great," I said. "Father and daughter working at the same publishing house."

"I'm a lawyer," said Timothy.

"Sorry?" I said.

"We're planning an intervention," said Cassandra. "For Leo. We're gathering information for it."

"How much is he doing?" Timothy said.

"I don't know," I said. "I don't really know the guy."

"He talked like you were close," said Cassandra.

"I'm not sure what to tell you," I said. "I'll help any way I can."

"Help yourself!" said Timothy. "Save yourself, young man. Dear God, go to your family. You are about to die. Don't you see this?"

"Sometimes," I said.

The man shook and crossed his arms.

"Daddy," said Cassandra. "Daddy, we can go now."

"What about the book?" I said.

"The book."

"The advance?"

"The advance," said Cassandra. "Here's your advance."

She pulled bills from her bag, tossed them onto the table.

"Pay for the drinks. Whatever is left is your advance. But don't ever contact me again. And stay away from Leo. Seriously. You are never to be in his presence again. My husband works for the district attorney. Don't cross me, or people will put you in the river. Let's go, Daddy."

My editor led her sobbing father away.

"One more thing," she called over her shoulder. "Boxing is barbaric, and you are a sick little parasite. What do you know about sweat and blood? Bet you've never even been punched in your life. I'm serious about Leo. Stay away!"

I scored down at Fanny Packs and headed back to the apartment. Gary and John and John's cousin had gathered on the futons.

"I saw your sister," I said to John's cousin.

"What the hell are you talking about?"

"You gave me her number."

"Right. For your book."

"I was robbed!" said Gary, giggling.

"He did lose one bout," I said to Gary. "Early in his career. Lost it fair and square. To Willie 'the Worm' Monroe. The Worm took him in Philly."

"The Worm!" cried Gary.

"The defeat was soon avenged," I said. "And here's one more thing, and then I'll shut up. They did an MRI on Hagler's skull. It was abnormally thick. It was basically a helmet."

"Cool," said John.

"My sister likes your idea?" said John's cousin.

"I don't think so. She's got some other things on her mind."

"Like what?"

"Like you."

"Me?"

"She's going to intervene. Your dad, too. They're planning the big ambush. They've got the maps out. They're watching you through scopes. Somebody will give the signal."

"What are you talking about?"

"You're Leo, right?"

"Of course I'm Leo."

"The van will pull up. Men will pour out. Or maybe your sister will just take you out for a nice meal. All the people you've ever felt judged by will be there."

"What?"

"You're going to rehab, Reverend."

"I was rehabbed!" said Gary.

"Shit," said John's cousin. "Not again."

"What about me?" said John.

"They didn't mention you," I said. "I think you're on your own."

Supplies ran low, and I went back to Fanny Packs. The big guy was gone. There was police tape across the doorway, a dark, wet splash on the wall. I hit other spots, blocks and blocks away, but they were closed. The Laundrymat: closed. Pillbox: closed. Rumpelstiltskin: closed. Scooter Rat was nowhere. Ditto the Old Lady of the Sealed Works. That left Cups.

Cups was near the river in a crumbly walk-up. The light was on in the hallway and I could see people huddled near the banister. I started up the stoop when a hand shot out and grabbed me.

"Hey."

He was a big kid, lumpy in the folds of his sweatshirt. He rubbed his stubble-covered head.

"I'm stuck here, bro," he said. "I'm on lookout. I need a bag, you know? Just buy me a bag while you're in there."

He pressed a ten-dollar bill into my hand.

"I don't know," I said.

"Yeah, you know. Just get me a bag."

"Boy?"

"What? Get me a bag of dope."

"Okay," I said, shrugged, went inside.

I waited behind a man who stank of subway station elevators and a soulful-looking woman in fishnet sleeves. The thing about Cups was you never saw the guys with the cups. They stayed upstairs, invisible puppeteers. The Styrofoam containers bobbed down on strings. The lookouts on the stoop and the rooftops called their codes, for the cops, for the all clear.

"*Gato!*" they'd shout, and I pictured jaguars with badges in their fur.

Maybe I pictured that now as the cups came down. I put the lookout's money in with mine in the cup marked D, watched it go up. The cup started down once more, but there was something wrong. The lookouts shouted, the cup swung hard, bounced off the stair rails, tilted, tipped. The lights went out.

I groped the scummed tiles for my bags. Broken bottles pricked my palms. I heard a burst of siren, then more shouting, then nothing at all. My hand brushed something, one of the tiny glassine envelopes. I scooped it into my fist. The lights came on. The lookout stood in the doorway.

"Got my bags?" he said.

"Bag," I said. "One bag. You only gave me ten dollars."

"I gave you twenty, motherfucker. You trying to rip me off?"

"No, man."

"You little fucking junkie, trying to rip me off. Just give me what you've got."

I walked toward him, opened my palm. We both sort of gasped when we saw the flattened cigarette butt.

"I'm sorry," I said. "I'm really sorry. I'm sure it's over there near the stairs. Come on, let's look."

I wanted the lookout to follow me the way a father would, reserve judgment until it was clear a misdeed had occurred, maybe the way my father used to follow me when I was a boy, for he was a reporter and his job was to seek the facts, even if it was just the fact of who won a ball game or who'd ripped the sofa or stained the rug. My father always wanted to know what was truly happening.

Except maybe once.

There had been a big snowfall, and we stood in the driveway we'd just cleared, leaned on our shovels, sucked icy air.

"I remember," my father said then. "I remember when you were a little boy. You had some words here and there, but you hadn't really spoken a sentence yet. We were all waiting for your big first sentence. We were eating dinner and I was having my wine. I get up for some bread and knock over the glass. Wine spills everywhere. Stains the tablecloth. You know how your mother was about stains. We're all sitting there afraid to speak, and you know what you said?"

"No."

" 'I'm sorry.' That's what you said. 'I'm sorry.' Hah. You were always like that."

"Like what?" I said.

"Listen," said my father. "I need to tell you something. I don't love your mother anymore. I'm seeing somebody else. Somebody I love. I care about you, but I can't live with your mother right now."

"She's really sick."

"I know. Believe me. That's what makes it so hard."

"You fucking bastard," I said.

"Okay," said my father. "I'm not going to let you speak to me like that too much. But right now is warranted. Give me what you got."

I stood there, stared at him.

"That was it?" said my father. "Come on, take a shot. Sock it to me. Haymaker express."

I cocked my fist, studied the salt bristles in his chin.

"Lay me out, baby," said my father. "Onetime offer. Put the old fuck on the deck. Don't be a damn pansy! I'm leaving your dying hag of a mother!"

I turned hard, took a few steps, and threw a huge hook at the garage door. We both heard my hand bones crack. I slid to the pavement, squealed.

"Oh, Christ," said my father. "No good deed."

He clutched me up and rolled me into the car, drove us to the hospital.

It was true about no good deed, or even bad deed, same as it was true about fathers and how they forget to love you, but it's more that they've forgotten everything.

Maybe it's just a classic American condition.

None of it mattered now. The lookout's eyes filled with this silvery hate and he gathered up the collar of my shirt and commenced what people who have never been punched, people like me, call fisticuffs. He threw hard, perfect crosses, and my legs fell away and the blows did not cease. I could feel them, not feel them, their smash and wreck, the splintering of bone, feel my blood, this warm, barbaric blood, so rich and parasitical, pour out my nose and sluice out my mouth and down my throat and choke me with the shock of something terrible and unendingly foreseen.

When he was done, the kid leered down at me.

"Had enough?" he said.

"Yes," I lied.

EXPRESSIVE

Folks say I have one of those faces. Not just folks, either. People say it. You have one of those faces, they say, a person can tell what you are feeling. Mostly what I'm feeling is that I've just farted, but I nod anyway, twitch up my eyes, my mouth, all earnest and merciful. It's called *Joy Is Here (So Don't Be Such a Prune-Hearted Prick)*, or at least that's what I call it. If you know how to work your face, you can make people think you feel anything you want, and with that power you can feel up anything you want.

Example: this chick, Roanoke, I meet at the Rover. She's kind of dykey, the way I like them, has her own darts for the dartboard.

I buy her a beer.

"You're kind of dykey," I say.

"Thanks," she says, in the tone of her generation.

Roanoke rolls the dart in her hand. I glance off, swivel back with *Harmless Fool / No Strings Attached / Penis as Pure Novelty*, which sounds easy but requires most of the human face's approximately seventy-three thousand muscles.

Next thing we're back in her efficiency and Roanoke's moaning with her hand on her mouth. She's worried we won't hear the door if the girlfriend comes home. We do hear the door, but that's not the problem. The problem is efficiency. The apartment is laid out perfectly for dykes to discover they've betrayed each other and their way of life. A curtain around the bed might help.

I give Roanoke one more look before I leave her to the business of ducking creamers, ramekins. I call it *Remember, the World Is Not Broken, Even If Your Crockery Is.*

Folks, people, like to ask what you would do in a moment of great moral confusion. Would you save that burning portrait of Hitler painted by Rembrandt? Who cares? The serious question is what are you doing right now. Do you have time for another drink?

My friend, or, rather, anti-friend, Ajay disagrees.

"You're an idiot," says Ajay.

"Go back to fucking Mumbai," I tell him. "Or whatever the fuck it's called now."

"Mumbai," says Ajay. "And I was born here."

"In the Rover?"

It's not a bad place to be born. Every third beer is a buy-back.

I don't bother pulling a face. They never work on Ajay, not even *I Know My Racism Amuses You, but It's Still Racism, so I Win*, and anyway it gets tiresome manipulating my universe. It's nice to give those millions of tiny face muscles a break. Ajay goes up to the bar, and I keep my eyes peeled for dart dykes. When he comes back, I tell him all about Roanoke.

"You really are a fucking idiot. Go home to your wife."

I go home to my wife. She's sitting up at the kitchen table with a mug of coffee, like she saw it in a movie about a wife sitting up for her shitty husband. She clicks her wedding ring against the side of the mug, which is my mug, a mug she gave me that reads WORLD'S SHITTIEST HUSBAND.

I tell her everything, but I can hardly hear my words because I'm focused on the nearly Dutch wonder forming on my face—*Most Radiant Penitence*. It's a fairly simple purse-and-squint combo, but unless performed by an old master like myself, it risks smirk.

"Motherfucker," my wife says, in the tone of an earlier generation. "Do you love her?"

"Not her," I say. "Maybe the one who caught us."

"I want to save our marriage," says my wife. "Do you want to save our marriage?"

"Yes," I say. "Just not right now."

"Get out."

I've got my prepacked get-out bag and I'm standing in the nursery doorway watching my sleeping son sleep. His face is smooth and milky in the moonlight, and there's really no name for it, his face, not yet, except maybe *I'm Sleeping*. Some people might consider this expression beautiful, but it scares the crap out of me. You need more than *I'm Sleeping* to navigate all the evil in this world. Me gone, who's going to teach my boy *The Strange Thing Is It's Nobody's Fault*, or *Believe I Jammed the Printer All You Want, We've Still Got to Order Toner*? Folks? People? My wife? I drop my get-out bag on the nursery floor, curl up next to the crib. There's the moon through the window, that Moon Man with his masterful Moon Man look: *We Are All Schmucks, but I Control the Tides*. If he had a coffee mug, it would read "World's Shittiest Moon." But he doesn't have a coffee mug. I get that now.

ODE to OLDCORN

Oldcorn was a shot-putter from the hippie days. He was my hero for a while. I was a shot-putter from the long-after-the-hippie-days-were-gone days. It was called the Reagan era, but I learned that only later.

We studied the Oldcorn Way with Coach Monroe. Old-corn torque, Oldcorn spin.

"Finish like this," said Coach Monroe. "Do not fall out of the circle. Your mark means nothing if you fall out of the circle. It's a foul. Do it enough times, you foul out. Like you were never even here."

We all nodded, me and Merk and Fred Powler, the police chief's son. We were the fattest, strongest boys in our school. We had nothing to do, nowhere to be. There's not a lot of call for our type until the weather gets cold.

"It's all a question of character," said Coach Monroe. "And fun. Fun's important."

We did wind sprints, stadium steps, pushed weights in the weight room. We'd sit out on the hill above the circle, roll shots in our hands. They were heavy things, seamed and bright, dusted with lime.

Coach Monroe sat with us, lotus-style, our guru. He gobbed down the ridge. He talked about Oldcorn, adjusted his balls. He had moods, tales to tell.

"Oldcorn dislocated his shoulder hundreds of times," he said. "It would pop out and he'd just pop it back in, step up for his next put.

"Oldcorn once said to me, 'Everything dies in the middle.' The put dies in the middle. Remember that. You can start hard and finish hard, but what did you do in the middle? Did you lapse? Was there a lapse? Did you think about Mindy Richter on the gymnastics team? Did you think about Mindy Richter hanging off those rings, her snapperhole all open and stinky-sweet? The put dies. End of story. Oldcorn got more cooze than you could keep between magazine covers under your bed next to your crusty sock. But do you know what he was thinking in the middle of his spin? Accelerate! Accelerate!

"I also want to tell you this: Oldcorn had black friends, Oriental friends, he had a Mexican roommate. That's character. It didn't matter what you looked like. He didn't care what was inside of you, either. He was a shot-putter. Now shower up."

We were fifteen, sixteen and maybe feeling funny when we showered up. We talked a lot about dropping the soap. Maybe Merk felt the funniest, but it wasn't his fault he had a foreskin, that his dong had weird veins. He was from a weird country. We taunted him, but only in the shower room.

"Hey," said Fred Powler. "What's a snapper?"

"What're you, a fucking 'tard?" said Merk.

"Leave him alone," I said.

Picture me, the good kid from after-school television. Picture Fred, the feeb who will teach us to be free. That's the story of humanity, or at least that was the story of Fred. He'd been smarter than any of us and not teaching us anything until some punk got Fred in the skull with a snowrock. An accident, said Fred's dad, Chief Powler. Most of the world's snowrocks are packed by accident, I'm sure. Now Fred maybe belonged on that bus with the rubber handles, but who had the heart to put him on it? I didn't have that kind of heart. I did Fred's homework for him. I figured he could start to be retarded next year.

Twilight, we'd walk home to our houses down streets named for famous soldiers: Eisenhower, Bradley, MacArthur, Mc-Queen. We had our own names for places that didn't have town names. I worried the feebed version of Fred had forgotten them all.

"What's that?" I said.

"It's for cars."

"The Parking Lot of Lost Ambition," I said. "And what's behind it?"

"Bushes."

"The Forest of Teen Pregnancy," I said.

That's maybe where Mindy Richter was right now, I added, conducting guided tours of her snapperhole. When I got to Oklahoma State, Oldcorn's alma mater, on my shot put scholarship, all the Mindy Richters of the world would beckon me from beds of silk. They'd wake at dawn, alone, a poem there on the pillow where my cheek had been.

An ode to Oldcorn, maybe.

There was a book in the library called *Athletes of the Seventies*. I spent a lot of study periods studying a photograph of Oldcorn in the middle of a spin. Sweat twirled off his antiwar whiskers. His mouth was cut wide with what must have been his famous banshee noises. The shot was pitted, chalked, cradled in the hollow of his neck. I could almost see it flying off his fingertips, hang there in the day skies of my mind, an iron moon.

We took a bus to a meet in the land of the Jackson Whites, a mountain people with too many fingers on their hands and even fingers on their feet. The Jackson Whites were a wild breed, Coach Monroe had told us, come down from Revolutionary War times—Hessian deserters, Indians, runaway slaves. There on the mountain they made their own inbred mutant race. I was hoping to see a flipper boy flapping on a banjo or a Revolutionary lute.

But this mountain had big houses on it. There were shiny cars with smug bumper stickers parked along the road. We drove up to a beautiful school, this tinted octagon of new-math glass. Our milers, quarter milers, hurdlers and high hurdlers, long jumpers and high jumpers and triple jumpers and pole-vaulters, all our twitchy golden Spartans jumped off the bus and ran up to the bleachers, the raked cinder track. There were no shot-putting circles in sight.

Coach Monroe grabbed a guy jogging past. The man's whistle popped from his lips.

"Where the hell do you put around here?"

"Put what?" said the man.

"The shot."

"Other side of the school," he said.

"Where? In the fucking woods?" said Coach Monroe. "These kids aren't lepers. In Europe, this sport is appreciated."

"Go throw in Europe," said the man.

"Put," said Coach Monroe. "Not throw."

We found the circle, a pack of boys warming up. They looked like us with better sneakers. They wore brand-new shorts with bright metallic trim. Coach Monroe took the tape measure out of his coat. There were not enough judges in this part of New Jersey. We would have to judge for ourselves.

Coach Monroe gathered us to him, jabbed his clipboard at each of our hearts.

"Go, Spartans!" said Merk.

"Forget that crap," said Coach Monroe. "Just accelerate."

It wasn't even what you would call a contest. The kids in the metallic shorts were gliders, like some lost clan of Cro-Mags, new to fire, ignorant of spin. They were good sports, though. They hopped around with the tape roll, called out our marks.

"Teach us that spin you do," one of them said.

"Are you a Spartan?" said Merk.

"We're Badgers," said the boy.

"They're Jacksons," I said.

"I'm a Baum," said the boy.

"Can't help you," said Merk. "It's the Spartan spin."

"It's Oldcorn's," I said.

"What's Oldcorn?" said Baum.

"Look it up," I said. "There's a book."

Somebody stared at us from the edge of the field. He had dirty pants, carried a planter and a spade. I tried to look into his crazy Jackson eyes, but there was nothing crazy about them. Just bored.

"That's the groundskeeper," said Baum.

"Oh," I said.

Sometimes after a big meet we went to Merk's uncle's house to drink beer. Merk's uncle's basement was filled with beer, beer memorabilia, electric beer signs, and beer embroidery on the wall. Merk's uncle worked in beverage distribution. Mostly beer. He said we could drink all we wanted, as long as we stayed in the basement.

There was a pool table down there. The cue sticks were just the right size for indoor javelin. We didn't have outdoor javelin at our school anymore. Some kid had caught one in the neck.

Now the basement door swung open and there were Merk's uncle's loafers on the top step.

"Hello, boys," he called. "I'm home and I'm thirsty. Pour one for the old man."

Last time he'd gotten drunk with us, he'd sung love ballads into a balled-up pair of underwear.

"I've got to book," I said.

Oldcorn won gold in Mexico. He was supposed to go to Munich, but he shattered his hip in a bike wreck. The hip never healed right. He had to revert to the glide. He won some meets, but he wasn't Oldcorn anymore. He went out for the American team in 1976, the Montreal games, but with one put left in the trials, trailing badly, Oldcorn walked off the field, disappeared.

"He went to an ashram," said Coach Monroe.

"Why?"

"Fuck if I know."

"What's an ashram?" I said.

Coach Monroe's office was a cubbyhole behind the basketball bleachers. His desk was heaped with binders, team rosters, meet schedules, pole vault catalogs. He lit a cigarette, took a puff, blew the smoke into a gym bag, zipped it shut. Then he dunked the cigarette in a cup of tea.

"There," he said. "Now, what were we talking about?"

"Oldcorn," I said.

"Well, what can I say? I don't know. He was an eccentric dude. He lived a private system. I know you guys like hearing about the good old days, but you should concentrate on what you're doing now. Which brings me to another question. What do you think you're doing now?"

"What do you mean, Coach?"

"Don't get me wrong. I like having you around. You're a nice kid. But how far do you think you're going with the shot put?"

"I don't know," I said. "I guess I never thought about it."

"That's good," said Coach Monroe. "That's good to hear."

Coach Monroe said there would be a special surprise at our last home meet. When those Jacksons, with their satchels and their magic shorts, made their way to our circle, I saw what he meant. The special surprise was named Bucky Schmidt. He was enormous, milky-blue colored, like thin milk, with a flat head and a mean Hessian nose. He was the most mutated boy you could ever hope to see, though you had to look hard to see the Jackson in him. Or maybe there wasn't any Jackson in him at all.

I do know the world is divided, or even just subdivided, between those who have met their Bucky Schmidt and those who have their Bucky coming. I've met my Bucky Schmidt and so I'm never disappointed by the way of things. I don't want and want. Good money, good times, I'm happy for what I get. You don't worry so much about it all when you know there is somebody out there who can take everything away like some terrible god.

That day, all of us just stood there to watch a god put shots. I wondered what Bucky Schmidt was thinking in the middle of his spin. I doubt it was snapperholes, or even to accelerate. The word "accelerate" would have slowed him down. The boy was pure blur.

"He's a strange guy, but holy shit," said that Badger, Baum. "And he throws longer in practice."

"He doesn't throw," I said.

"What?"

"It's not throwing. It's putting. Shot-putting."

"Sure thing," said the Badger.

"Have you looked at his toes?" I said.

"Why would I do that?"

"Does he have a banjo?"

"Clarinet. I've seen it."

"Can he talk?"

"Why wouldn't he talk?"

"He's a Jackson, right?" I said.

"He's a Schmidt," said the Badger. "Is that a Jackson? What's a Jackson?"

"Ask Schmidt," I said.

After the meet, Coach Monroe gathered us next to the field house.

"I want to thank you boys for a great year," he said. "You really gave it your all."

"We got killed today," said Merk.

"You sure as hell did," came a voice.

A stranger leaned on the field house wall.

"Guys," said Coach Monroe. "I'd like you to meet Rick Oldcorn. The one and only."

This Oldcorn was as huge as I'd always imagined, but bald, with muttonchop whiskers and a gut that buried his belt. He wore cop shades, a T-shirt for a titty bar. He looked like a Jackson, or what I figured a Jackson would look like if I ever really saw one. Maybe I never would.

"You guys are shit," said Oldcorn, "but what can you do with a jackass like Monroe for a coach?"

"Thanks, pal," said Coach Monroe, and his smile said it all, though I wasn't exactly sure what it said.

"Let's get out of here," said Oldcorn.

"Do you want beer?" said Merk.

"I want all the beer in your town," said Oldcorn. "And I want teen poot, if that's available. Let's ride."

We piled into Coach Monroe's pickup. Oldcorn followed on his bike. Soon we sat in Merk's uncle's basement drinking beer and sword fighting with cue sticks. It was fun for a while. Fun was important.

"You guys want a bump?" said Oldcorn, pulling out a small packet.

"Do your arm!" said Fred Powler.

Oldcorn grinned, popped his shoulder out of its socket, popped it back.

Then Merk's uncle came down with more beer.

"We can do whatever we want," he announced, "as long as we stay in the basement."

Soon he was crooning into a spatula.

Fred Powler lay down on the pool table. "Lost ambition," he said. "For cars."

Slivers of puke clung to his lip.

Merk carried his uncle up to bed. Coach Monroe slumped in the corner. Oldcorn and I sat at the bar with our beers. It felt like a place I would be for a long time to come.

"Why did you walk off the field in the trials for Montreal?" I said.

"I met this chick," he said.

"Oh."

"No, that's not it."

"Then what?"

"I don't know. It all got damn depressing. Going from town to town just to throw a metal ball around. Seemed silly."

"Put," I said. "Not throw."

"Jesus, kid," said Oldcorn. "Don't be one of those guys."

"But you were the best in the world," I said.

"Damn straight I was," said Oldcorn. "So you can imagine the scope of my depression."

"Up yours," said a voice behind us. "Up yours, Oldcorn."

Coach Monroe steadied himself on a beer lamp, rose.

"Hey, good buddy," said Oldcorn. "Welcome back."

"Up yours, you, buddy," said Coach Monroe. His eyes had wet, pulsing rims.

"Oldcock," said Coach Monroe.

"Watch it, now," said Oldcorn.

"Oldfuck."

It was all pretty quick. Coach Monroe had a beer bottle he was maybe thinking of cracking over Oldcorn's head. Next thing he was on his knees, pawing for his nose through the blood on his face.

Oldcorn rubbed his fist.

"Tell that other kid thanks for the beer."

I heard his bike start up on the gravel drive.

I do not know if Oldcorn found any teen poot that night. It might not have been so available. We heard nothing about him and did not speak of him again.

Coach Monroe wore gauze on his nose for the rest of the year. He went on to marry Mindy Richter's mother.

Merk went off to the war. I haven't talked to him since graduation, when we all walked down the stadium steps in our nylon robes and got certificates for being alive and living in New Jersey—all of us except Fred Powler, who didn't quite qualify, but who waved to us from the grass.

I wish there was some other story that could make you feel better about Fred Powler, but he clubbed his father with a chair leg and had to go to some kind of home. Chief Powler claimed it was an accident, which I'm sure it was.

Everything in this life, with the exception of snowrocks, is an accident.

I live in the city now. There are so many kinds of people here, and sometimes they look at me funny, like I've just come down from a shack on a mountain. But I've got a studio apartment. There's just enough room for some good spins on the hardwood. I'll spend Sunday morning being Bucky Schmidt, or the Oldcorn of Mexico, gun grapefruits into the wall. My last girlfriend used to get pissed when I did this, plus they were her grapefruits, but what the hell, she was over me anyway.

THIS APPOINTMENT OCCURS in the PAST

Davis called, told me he was dying.

He said his case was—here was essence of Davis—time sensitive.

"Come visit," he said. "Bid farewell to the ragged rider."

"You?" I said. "The cigarette hater? That's just wrongness."

"Nonetheless, brother, come."

"Who was that?" said Ondine, my ex-mother-in-law. I kissed her cream-goldened shoulder, slid out of bed.

"A sick friend. I've known him twenty years, more, since college. I might have to leave town for a while."

"No," said Ondine. "You're leaving town for good. The occupation ends today. It's been calamity for us, for the region. Go to your friend."

"He's not really my friend."

"All the more reason to go to him," said Ondine. "Jesus would be in Pennsylvania by now."

Ypsilanti was easy to leave. I wasn't from there. I'd just landed there. The Michigan Eviscerations had begun in Manhattan. Martha was a junior at NYU, heiress to a fuel-injection fortune. I was the cheeky barista who kept penciling my phone number on her latte's heat sleeve. Cheeky and, I should add, quite hairy. Martha finally dialed the smudged figures on the corrugated cuff, cavorted in my belly fur. The woman never exhibited any qualms about our economic divide. After all, she'd remind me, I was a Jew. One day I'd just quit mucking around with burlap sacks of Guatemalan Sunrise and start brewing moolah.

"You can't help it," she said. "It's a genetic thing. You weren't allowed to own land in the Middle Ages."

I wasn't allowed to own land in Michigan either. We got married, but her folks bought the Ann Arbor house in her name. Martha enrolled for a master's degree at the university. She demanded that I concoct a passion she could bankroll, a "doable dream." What would it be? Poetry journal? Microlabel for the new jam rock? Nanobatch raki boutique? I mulled over these and other notions but mostly focused on my favored pursuit: grilling premium meats. I grilled grass-fed beef, saddles of rabbit, bison, organic elk. My mulled projects moldered. I'd always pictured myself the genius *in* the journal, *on* the label, not running the damn things. Moreover, wasn't there bookkeeping involved, basic math? No matter what Martha believed about my inherited numerical wizardry honed on the twisty streets of Antwerp, or maybe Münster, I could barely count.

I grilled until the grilling season ended. Around the time the first shipment of Danish birch arrived for my new curing shed, Martha kicked me to what in this municipality wasn't quite a curb. She'd met an equally hirsute Scot from the engineering school. His name happened to be Scott, and his people had the twisty brain too. Besides, our sex life was a wreck. We were down to those resentful tugs and frigs. She said the stench of burnt meat put her off. I figured it was also the weight I'd put on, the perpetual slick of cook grease on my chest beneath my loose kimono.

Ondine, an old beauty with hair the color of metallic marmalade, was historically attuned to her daughter's fecklessness. She took pity, rented me a unit in a shingle-stripped Victorian she owned in Ypsilanti, let me slide on the rent until I found a job. I never did, but she seemed satisfied to visit a few times a week for my attentions. She called my style of lovemaking "poignant."

Still, even before Davis called, I could tell she was getting bored.

"I'm getting bored," she said.

It came to her suddenly, unbidden, the way it might strike you that you hadn't gone candlepin bowling or eaten smoked oysters in years.

"You bore the piss out of me," she said.

I stood, started to dress.

Ondine reached out, pinched my ass fuzz.

"Ouch."

"Don't be so sensitive. Lots of things bore me. Things I love. My husband. My house. My daughter. My Native American pottery collection. It's not an insult."

But if not an insult, it was a signal. Now, weeks later, I headed east in one of Ondine's several Mazdas, a parting gift, along with a generous cash severance and a few keepsake snapshots of her in aspects of the huntress.

The dashboard robot in the Mazda goaded. Beneath its officious tones I sensed confusion, a geopositional wound. Had some caustic robot daddy made it feel directionless? Meanwhile, the comics on the satellite radio joked about their dainty white cocks. Such candor was supposed to prevent the race war.

My neck ached, and I bought an ice pack, wedged it up against my headrest. My tongue was a mess. I still tasted Ondine. Deep in Pennsylvania I ate a coq au vin quesadilla. It's what Jesus would have ordered, and it was delicious.

I had to drive fast, before I ate too much road food.

The ragged rider, Davis had called himself, but I couldn't parse the phrase. I was naturally undetective.

Clues clenched me up.

I'd booked a tiny room in the Hudson Lux in New York City, high up and hushed, a loneliness box of polished walnut and chrome. You could picture yourself dead of a hanging jackoff in such a room, your necktie living up to its name, your lubricated fingers curled stiff near your hips. I stretched out on the narrow bed, decided not to picture this. It wasn't the kind of thing I figured I'd ever try. Aficionados cited the bliss spasm caused by air loss, but I wondered if most got orgasmic on the gamble. Anyway, everything in my life was a gamble, a wager that somebody would see to my needs. Was I secretly here because I thought Davis would somehow fit the bill even though he was sick? If so, who was sicker?

Now I shut my eyes, and Davis loped into view. He stood in an orchard of pomegranates, his legs greaved in low, personal mist. Tall, homely Davis, with his hamster fluff hair and granny specs.

We used to sip espressos in the campus café. Davis would read from his critical works: "In truth, of which there can be no certainty, the Peter Frampton phallus must be unfurled from the constrictive denim of manufactured desire's sweatshop."

I loved his papers, these phrases that seemed to trickle out of a plastic port under his shirt or hiss from slits in his hands. I wasn't one of those narcissists who thought I had to understand something for it to be important. Besides, he wasn't wrong about whatever the hell he meant.

He wasn't wrong about much. I rarely went to lectures. Davis tutored me.

We drank beer in the old sailor's bar and Davis would whisper about the Russians—Pushkin, in particular, whose story "The Shot" he so admired.

"Pushkin invented Russian literature as we know it," he said.

"But I don't know it," I said.

Davis studied Latin, computers, knew some physics, dabbled in questions that plagued those he sneeringly called the string cheese theory people. He taught me to marvel at the elegance of Nagle's law and the Peck conjecture, though maybe they had other names. Even words associated with counting undid me.

We slurped whiskey in our basement apartment with our friends and possible friends. Davis was the savior. I was his handsome disciple. Eventually Davis would get huffy about the cigarette smoke and stomp around the piles of books and laundry, the stray Stratocaster, the tripod with the liquid swivel. We were making an experimental video for our band, the Interpellations, but who wasn't?

"How can you breathe in corporate death like that!" Davis shouted one night. "Smoke the kind, like me."

"We're not hippies," said Caldwell, neobeat goblin. "I'll take the bourbon of my fathers."

"But this is the one thing the hippies got right!" Davis said, held aloft his cinnamon-scented bong. "Maybe they sold out the working class, but they grooved! Anyway, there are too many of them. So few of us. They will rule our lives forever. They will never pass the torch."

"Do we deserve it?" I said. I guess I'd gotten tired of being his disciple.

"I do," said Davis.

"So what kind of ruling-class motherfucker are you," I said, "to be talking about the torch?"

I knew this would bother him. He'd been born into citrus

money. We'd get crates of tangelos delivered to our door. Also, his girlfriend, the Brilliant Brianna, which was her official nickname, had made some late-night sojourns to my ashy mattress. Davis starred in the Invention of Monogamy seminar, so his hands were tied, so to speak, but I could tell he seethed.

"Be nice," Brianna mouthed now, but I plowed on, foolishly, for her, I imagine. I was not yet heart literate.

"Davis," I said. "Davis."

"What is it, Sasha, my brother?"

"My name isn't Sasha."

"Is it something?"

"Davis," I said. "You've grown clownish. I'm sure you're right about the cigarettes. But you're not our father."

"I don't believe in fathers," said the goblin Caldwell. "Except my bourbon fathers. Listen to Sasha."

"Davis sucks," called a girl near the stereo. "Sasha, or whatever, is our hero. Ask Brianna."

Brianna ducked her head, but Davis caught her eye. He threw her an evil glance as he departed. We stayed, drank, smoked, forgot bad things. We laughed. We stood up and sat down. We impersonated each other standing up and sitting down. We told tedious stories about our childhoods, feigned enthrallment. That part of the evening arrived when people sat closer together on the carpet. One groupuscule, a reedy boy and two brawny women, groped and giggled, mashed their faces for a trilateral smooch. Brianna and I fell entwined into the couch.

"What makes you think you're smart enough to talk to him like that?" she whispered, tongued my ear. "You're just a dumb piece of gash. We like you for your innocent enthusiasm. Remember that."

"I will."

"No, you won't."

That's when Davis returned with his velvet-lined mahogany pistol case. A brace of Berettas gleamed from their notches: compacts, pearl handled, gold flecked. We broke our clinches as Davis called the room to attention.

"Big happenings, entertainment-wise, folks. Gather round for what will prove a violent and transformative highlight of your lives."

"Guns?" called a tall fellow with a can of dip. He was a theater jock from Texas, which meant he affected flasks and went bare chested under his pleather vest.

"Put those away," said Brianna. "Davis, this is not funny."

"It's just a game. They're not loaded."

"What game?" said Brianna.

"Come, Princess," he said to me. "I mean, Countess. Choose one."

"You're drunk," said Brianna.

"Somewhat. Also stoned. Why do we even say stoned? So brutal. So Levitical. Pick a pistol, dreamboy. We're going to play out that scene for our friends here. From the Pushkin."

"And then will you can it?" I said.

"Like Steinbeck."

"Goddamn ridiculous." I hardly looked at the pistols, drew one from the box, took a position near the stereo. The girl who stood there smirked.

"They're not loaded," I said.

"Bummer."

I shrugged, raised the pistol at Davis.

"Did I grant you first shot?" said Davis.

"I'm following the story. I'm the young, handsome soldier everyone has left your orbit to be near. You are the older, bitter officer who can't compete with my charisma."

"Funny," said Davis. "Not exactly as I saw it, but I admire

your hustle. You framed the scene first. We'll go with your version."

"It all fits, Davis. You called for the duel. You're the crack shot. I've never even fired a gun."

"True. Well, on with it, then. You may have the first metaphorical shot, you upper-crust social usurper. Just flick that safety off."

"What about the tangelos?"

"My poor father has a little tree. Now take your shot."

Our audience, stymied in their lust, groaned at our stage-craft.

I grinned and pulled the trigger. Davis fell back with the bang. There was a neat hole in the drywall.

"Shitsnickers!" called the kid with the dip.

Brianna swayed in shock. The goblin squealed under the table, and the girl by the stereo clutched her ears.

Powder smoke hung in a clot. The room hummed with vanished noise. We stood there, grave and giddy.

I shook, and laid the pistol on the coffee table. My stomach cramped, and I wanted a cigarette. I wanted to see the body. I started to move, but Davis popped up, waved his Beretta.

Brianna swooped in and wrapped him in her arms.

"Baby," he cried. "Was that dramatic? Was it worthy?"

"Are you hurt?"

"Not a scratch! How did it look?"

"It was radically trangressive," she said. "Of something."

Davis nuzzled his lady, shoved her away.

"Now we must complete this man deed."

"No," said Brianna. "No, sweetie. The piece landed perfectly. Don't fiddle."

"It's okay," I said, lighting a Korean cigarette I'd mooched from a pack on the table.

"It is?" said the girl by the stereo.

"Davis'll put one in your frontal cortex," said the Texan.

"No, he won't," I said.

"You going to duck it like Davis?" said the goblin.

"Just watch."

Davis hocked a loogie and leveled his gun. The room got quiet. Davis winked, lowered the Beretta.

"No, no," he said with the quiet and cadence of a maestro. "I think I'll take my shot another day. I think I'll wait. Until our friend here is a little older. When he's lost his bunnylike nihilist strut. When he's discovered love. When he's struck a truce with feeling. When his every thought and action isn't guided by childish terror. When he's graduated from douchebaggery. When he truly understands all that he's about to lose. Let's forget these shenanigans for now. Just a little show. But you, buddy of my heart, you'd best watch the ridges and the roads. It could be years from now, but watch for the ragged rider's approach. He comes only for his shot."

"And . . . scene," I said. We'd taken some drama classes together. The others clapped hard for our skit, or the oratory, really. Davis, wasted in the right ratios, was a natural. We both took a bow.

I had one of those phones that did everything, but I could never master the simplest apps. Every time I tried to add to my schedule, these words would flash on the calendar display: "This appointment occurs in the past." I grew to rely on the feature. It granted me texture, a sense of rich history.

I was remarking on this to Davis in the midtown diner where we'd agreed to meet. I suppose you could call it a retro diner, but what diner isn't? They're all designed to make you think fried food won't kill you because it's the 1950s and nobody knows any better, and besides, there's a chance you haven't been born yet.

We dug into our bacon and cheddar chili burgers. I watched Davis chew.

He didn't look sick at all. He was still ugly but a good deal less so. Some men get handsome later. It's up to them to make it count. He'd replaced his granny glasses with modish steel frames. He looked scientific, artistic, somebody trained to talk to astronauts about their dreams. He eyed me over his drippy meat.

"That's funny," he said. "I could look at your phone, maybe fix it."

"No," I said. "I like it that way."

We were silent for a moment.

"So," I said. "The ragged rider."

"Indeed."

"You look fantastic. I thought you'd be much more winnowed."

"It's not that kind of disease."

"What kind is it?"

"We're still working on that. The doctors."

"I'm sorry. Whatever it is."

"It's in the blood. They know that. I'm sorry, too. But at least it's given me an excuse to gather my old friends."

"We haven't talked since—"

"Since graduation," said Davis.

"No," I said. "That other time."

We'd run into each other in a cocktail lounge in San Francisco several years after college. Davis wore a suit of disco white and toasted the would-be silicon barons at his table. I, assistant manager of this spacey blue sleazepit for the young and almost rich, sloshed Dom in their flutes. Davis slipped me some cash and a wink, but he flailed in a world beyond his code capacity. His group appeared composed of algorithmic gangsters, expert wielders of their petty and twisty Jewish, Welsh, Cambodian, Nubian, and Mayan brains. They hadn't spent their undergraduate years soused, brandishing pistols and theory. They'd been those morose, slightly chippy bots I'd noticed at the refectory whenever I rolled in for some transitional pancakes after a night of self-bludgeoning. They were churls with huge binders, and I'd always known they were my betters.

"Be honest," said Davis at the bar. "Are you gunning for maître d' or is this research for a screenplay?"

"I'm trying to pay my rent, sycophant."

"We were like brothers."

"Cain and the other one."

"That's true. So what's your life plan?"

"Drinking," I said. "One day at a time."

"These people here think I'm Swiss," said Davis. "They think I have Ph.D.s in cognitive science and computer engineering. There's a serious tip involved if you help maintain my cover."

"What's the angle?"

"I need them to work for stock options. I've got a start-up. It's called the Buddy System Network. You become friends with people online, share your opinions, your stories, put up pictures. Only connect, right? What do you think?"

"I think you're a freaking crackpot. Your idea is ludicrous. People aren't machines."

"If you'd read more great literature, you'd know that machines are exactly what people are."

Now, as we sat in the diner, Davis—the new, dying, steely, reframed Davis—dragged a waffle fry through his chili burger sauce.

"So what have you been doing?" I said, thoughtless as usual.

"Right now I seem to be dying. Before that I was looking

to break into your line of work. Sponging off wealthy women. My tangelo flow isn't what it used to be. The economy mugged the Davis dynasty. Come to my place tomorrow, will you? It would mean a lot to me."

That night, back in my shimmering crypt, I called Martha in Michigan.

"This is crazy," I said. "Let's patch it up."

"You turd, I'm married again."

"Oh, right," I said. "Scott. How well does he grill?"

"We're vegans now."

"No dairy?"

"Kills the sex drive."

"So that's what it was."

"No, honey, it was other things with us."

"How's your mom?"

"Let's not revisit that incident."

"Incident? Try era."

"I've got to go."

Down in the hotel bar, I thought of how much Davis and I still had to discuss. Our friendship, for example, and how quickly we'd passed through each other, from fascinated strangers to loyal chums to relics of each other's worlds. We'd been pawns of proximity, choiceless as brothers. I'd always sort of hated him, really, his arrogance, his masks, his whispery fake ways with my mind. I'd been nothing to him, just his handsome stooge, a barker for his depraved tent.

Now, I could tell you my family history and you could do some amateur noodle prods, conclude I needed one such as Davis to salve my certain hurts. Was it the time my mother beat my hands with a serving spoon while I stood enchanted by the ripples in her gray rayon blouse? Or the occasion my father recited a limerick that began "There once was a dumb fucking boy / who was never his daddy's joy"? Yes, we could solve for why, but we could also eat another slice of coconut cake. *Why* won't save you, anyway. *Why* makes it worse. And Davis, I realized, he wasn't sick.

He was sick.

I took the train and then the bus to his place in Red Hook. He lived in a refurbished ink factory. I pushed through the iron doors and climbed the stairs until I saw a metal plate with Davis's name on it. This building, he'd told me at the diner, was owned by rich artists who rented cheap, unsafe spaces to poor artists. Davis had a good deal with these slumlord aesthetes.

His apartment, empty and unlocked, was a great cement room with high windows. Greasy carpets covered the floor. A pair of half-shredded cane chairs and a stained divan connoted a parlor. I recognized all the furniture from the old days. He'd added nothing. Even the stereo had survived.

Davis appeared in his doorway. "Everyone's up on the roof, kid. Follow me."

He led me up a narrow ladder to a nearly nautical hatch. I popped through after him, my chin at tar level, surveyed the roof scene—so many pasty, dulled versions of the people I'd known, our old audience, and strangers, too. Caldwell the goblin had gone waxen and squinty. The Texan, dipless, had a tidy potbelly. He sported a polo shirt and unsevere trousers, golf philanthropical. The girl who once stood by the stereo was now a woman who hovered near a hooded grill. It resembled a Greek design I'd coveted from catalogs back in Ypsilanti. I could smell the seared tuna smoke, the zuke-juice vapors. Davis pulled me from the hatch, led me to the sawhorse bar. We had vistas of city and sea.

"My friend will have the rum punch," said Davis to the teen boy with the ladle.

"Okay, Dad."

Davis pounced on my surprise.

"You bet your life I have a magnificent son. This is Owney. Eugene Onegin Davis."

"A pleasure."

"You're doing the math, but I'll save you the trouble. Especially you. She drifted away from both of us that fateful night. But we crossed paths in Marfa years later."

"She?"

"She," said a voice. A dark, glitter-dusted hand brushed my shoulder: Brianna.

"So, you two are . . ."

"God, no," said Brianna. She still had the heart-threshing looks, the wicked corneal glint of a serious reader. "We still care for each other, and we both love Eugene, but our affections have relocated."

"Well phrased," said Davis.

"So," I said. "How are you dealing with the illness?"

Brianna looked baffled.

"Great news," said Davis. "I'm not terminal. That's you, I'm afraid. I'm going live forever. I've gotten my hands on some black market Super Resveratrol. I'll tell you, some of these scientists become dope slingers just to keep their three houses going. But no, I'm fine. How was I going to get you out here? For my shot?"

"Your what?"

"Please, you've already figured it out, I'm sure. Down deep"—he poked my chest bone—"you must have understood exactly what was going on."

"I don't have much of a deep down."

"But remember, this can't work unless you know what you will be missing."

"The future?" I said, and broke from his grip.

"What can't work?" said Brianna.

"Nothing, sweetie."

"Brilliant Brianna," I said. "Did you know I was married? The union didn't last. I couldn't forget you. I sexed it with the mother, though. That was tender."

"See, that song won't pass the audition," said Davis. "I have to know I'm ventilating a contented man. Otherwise it's a mercy job. So you've drifted a bit. Lived with uncertainty. You're a student of life. You're the eternal student. You should have lived centuries ago in Germany. Besides, you're a stud, my man. Women want to make love to your sunglasses. It's always been that way. You've pursued and overtaken happiness. Maybe you'll suddenly decide to make a ton of money, find a beauty to bear your children. This life, it's all so exalted, so tremendous and full of wonder, and also relaxing. Are you with me?"

"I've just been running from anything that resembled revelation. For twenty years I've been running."

"Nonsense," said Davis. "You have friends. You have health."

"I did quit the cowboy killers," I said. "And you and me, we had a ball, just hanging out, talking."

"I didn't like you," said Davis. "Go another way."

I stepped forward and stroked his lapels. He shucked me off.

"You condescended," said Davis. "Acted like you were killing time until a better life came along."

"You never cared for my ideas," I said, and snatched his hand, kissed his knuckles.

"What ideas?"

"Not ideas. Something. I've blocked most of it. Our whole friendship is a blur."

"I remember every microsecond," said Davis.

"It's really good to see you," I said.

"Fetch the party favor, Owney."

The boy reached under the bar for the mahogany box. Davis lifted out the Beretta.

"We'll just need one of these."

The new guests, who had gathered in for our sloppy matinee, gasped. The old hands, the repeat attendees, stood back.

"Not this homoerotic gunplay again," said the goblin.

"Homosocial," said Brianna. "Or, no, you're right."

"Shitesnickers," said the Texan, whom I'd overheard talking about his Irish roots.

"Just blanks," said the goblin. "They're old farts now. Wouldn't dare."

"It's a prank," a man with a gray-blond beard said to his date. "They all went to college together and it's like a sketch they do."

"Juvenile, entitled," said the date.

"It's like that Chekhov play," said another woman. "The one with the gun that must go off if you dare introduce it."

"No," the woman by the grill cried, wrapped herself around my waist. "Didn't you know it was me! Me all along!"

"Me who?" I said.

"Debbie!"

Brianna giggled, blew me a French kiss. It mattered that she'd never loved me, or ever saw me as anything but a pleasant face to mount. I'd always known this, but never understood how germane it was to what I'd begun calling, suddenly, inanely, my life narrative, which I assumed would culminate in our bright joining.

But here was Debbie instead.

"Debbie!" said Davis to me. "Yes! Of course. Your reason to live, pal! Debbie! The tragic element of your demise."

Davis pointed his oiled Lombardic hole puncher and took aim, as he had years before, when I had the soul of a laboratory coke mouse, craved only life's jolt, couldn't know wise joy.

"Debbie, honey," I whispered. "Move away. I'll be with you in a moment."

I raised my arms and tilted my head in the manner of the carpentered carpenter.

"And now, ladies and gentlemen, to complete a procedure begun many, many years ago, when I, Standish James Davis, having been fired upon by this knave during the latter days of Bush the Elder, take, as my duelist's right, the second and, fate willing, final shot of this contest. Furthermore—"

"Cap his monkey ass!" shouted Brianna.

Davis obliged.

Summertime, the neighbors come around to the backyard of the sweet rickety house Ondine sold us, watch me wheel up to the grills and baste the meats and flip them into Styrofoam boxes and thermal bags. We do only takeout, pork or beef, with biscuits and pop, and only on the weekend. We don't even have an official name, but I hear some people call our operation the Capo's, because a rumor floated that I was once some edge player in the North Jersey mob, got marked for a whack. Hence the wound, the wheelchair.

These are good people, but they watch too much television. Debbie, who works the register and is my wife, insists we do without one. We pass long evenings in our house drinking tea and talking about books and art and politics, or watching old movies on the computer, or having gentle, atrocious sex.

Sometimes Ondine comes over for poker or we all go out

for chimichangas. Last time, after a few drinks, I asked Ondine about her daughter.

"Martha? She'll never be happy with anybody but herself."

"Lucky girl."

"You lucked out, too," said Ondine.

"I know," I said. "But life gets really murky sometimes."

"It's true, honey. Like a fish tank nobody cleans. Just fish shit and dead fish. But that's how you know it's life."

Debbie is a big deal over at the university, where she got a professorship as soon as I was healed enough to marry. We didn't plan on Ypsilanti, but Michigan happened to want her. Sometimes I read her presentations for typos, but I don't understand them. Turned out she was the brilliant one of our bunch.

I never charged Davis, and they ruled the shooting an accident. If I'd charged him, I could have taken him to civil court and gutted him, but he wasn't lying about the disappearance of his family fortune. Last I heard, he ran some kind of permanent luau up on that Red Hook roof, and also a break-dancing camp for private school kids. Brianna, somebody told me, makes films of women giving birth alone in public spaces. I never even knew she liked that sort of thing.

I'm not sure why Debbie stays with me. Her devotion must have fixed itself to the memory of my brief, illusory splendor, or else she has some plan of revenge for the years I missed her charms. I would deserve that, if only because I know in my heart that if she were the ruined one, I would not stay.

It turns out you can live, even prosper, with that kind of truth. Until, I presume, you cannot.

I still wonder why our reenactment of that Pushkin story meant so much to Davis. My real confession is that I never even read the thing. Davis just told it to me. And the way he did so, now that I recall his manner, makes me suspect he hadn't read it, either.

Typical, I guess. We were poseurs, but why do you think poseurs pose? Because they want to be invited to the dominion of the real, an almost magical zone of unselfed sensation, and they know their very desire for it disqualifies them. Consider that, the next time you cluck your tongue at some awful, grandiose fake.

Dude just wants to feel.

I did almost achieve that sensation, or a cheater's version of it, but it had not much to do with Davis, or the rest.

It happened the night before I went to Red Hook, while I sat at the bar in the Hudson Lux. A woman took the next stool. She wore a silk dress with pearls, ordered one of those something-tinis. We introduced ourselves, but she had a thick accent and I couldn't make out her name.

"You a hairy motherfucker," she said, caressed my forearm where I'd rolled my sleeve.

"You want to see all of it?" I said.

Her room was just like my room, with more moon in the window.

We were on the bed when she asked the big New York, or at least Hudson Lux, question.

"What do you do?"

"I'm a barista by training," I said. "Though I enjoy grilling. I've also been a schoolteacher and worked construction and run the night shift at a homeless shelter and interned at a men's magazine."

"You here on business?"

"Are you here on business?" I said.

"You mean right now?"

"Yes," I said.

"Yes," she said. "What do you want?"

"Well, part of me just wants to die, but the other part wants to live, to really live."

"Okay," she said.

I slipped my belt off slowly, slung it from a hook in the door, looped.

It all followed rather quickly after that, a surge of bliss, a great groinal shudder, a shell burst of froth and light. Then I got cold, fogged. I floated in a bitter-tasting cloud, but in that moment I also glimpsed everything that was good and sweet and fresh, and also incredibly refreshing and relaxing, and I saw how I could reach that place and remain there for a very long time. After that, I think, somebody clutched my legs, my knees, shoved me upward, and a bald man with an earpiece and a combat knife cut me down from the door.

PEASLEY

The man who killed the idea of tanks in England—his afterlife.

—F. Scott Fitzgerald, *The Crack-Up*

The Man Who Killed the Idea of Tanks in England sipped tea in his parlor somewhere in England. Pale light trickled through the parlor's leaded windows in that trickling manner of English light as pictured by a person who would not know. The Man Who Killed the Idea of Tanks in England was an old man now. He passed his days sipping tea in his parlor and staining his mustaches with smoke from his briar pipe. His legs, once strong enough to spur his horse at a Boer sniper's nest or leap a boulder to avoid the whirling blades of a Mahdi charge, lay withered beneath the double layer of his tweed trousers and his dear dead wife's favorite shawl.

It was difficult to believe it was 1983. How old was he? One hundred and twenty-five? He had lived to see so much, from the murder of the czar to the Austrian paperhanger to the American moon shot, not to mention those urchins with the safety pins through their eyebrows and their so-called music.

The Sex Pistols were the best of the lot.

Still and all, it would be better to die now. It seemed to him during these days of pale, pictured light that the only thing keeping him out of his coffin was an unanswered question: Why had he killed the idea of tanks in England? He had had his reasons and recalled them quite well, thank you. Tanks were clunky. Tanks were slow. Tanks looked silly compared with, for instance, a mounted detachment of the Scots Guards cresting a hill on a crisp autumn day. Yes, he had been there when Mr. Simms demonstrated his "motor-war car," that boiler on wheels with the revolving Maxim guns. Impressive to a simpleton, perhaps, all those moving parts in the Daimler engine.

The light trickling through the leaded windows was certainly pale. This Public Image Limited business was a horrific mistake. Lydon had gotten it right the first time. The Man Who Killed the Idea of Tanks in England had gotten it wrong, stood there on that muddy field, snorted in Mr. Simms's expectant face.

"Won't do. Won't do at all."

Was he supposed to be some seer, then? A Delphic oracle? How could he predict such intractability, the endless trenches, all that wire, the Boche guns shredding so many tender poets? Surely he should be forgiven for killing the idea of tanks in England. Others, after all, had revived the idea, fetched it from conceptual purgatory. A little late to save the poets, perhaps, but there were too many anyway. Besides, who is to say they would not have roasted inside those infernal kettles?

Then again, with a jump on the job, England might have had a whole fleet of armored poet-preserving machines. Maybe one would have rolled over Corporal Hitler in No Man's Land, saved everyone a considerable inconvenience. Still, would that have been worth the price of watching Rupert Brooke die of prostate cancer?

It was the American Century, after all, or so the Americans kept proclaiming, and maybe they had a point. Though not much of a book fancier, the Man Who Killed the Idea of Tanks in England had always been keen on the Yanks. His favorite was the golden lush from Minnesota. *Gatsby* was tops. A secret part of him had always wished he could write such a bloody good novel. Or better yet, be the subject of a tale by such a blazing talent. But the story of the Man Who Killed the Idea of Tanks in England would probably never have occurred to Fitzgerald. The Man Who Killed the Idea of Tanks in England had spent most of the so-called Jazz Age pretending he had not killed the idea of tanks in England. It was not much of a story, was it?

It could very well have been that the Man Who Killed the Idea of Tanks in England was actually one hundred and twenty-seven years old. There were no papers pertaining to his birth. A bastard, he was, born in a hedgerow to a chambermaid. His father, the fake earl, had been kind enough to pay for schooling, after which the army seemed a natural choice. Leap a Sudanese boulder, charge some Boers, you might dodge certain questions of lineage. You might rise through the ranks until you have won enough medals to be asked your opinion of the idea of tanks in England.

Be ready, by God.

Now the Man Who Killed the Idea of Tanks in England heard the sound of an engine revving out past the garden. The Man Who Killed the Idea of Tanks in England peered out the parlor window. It was that damned Peasley, the groundskeeper, on his new contraption, the mechanized lawn mower. Peasley had eaten up a good deal of the grounds budget with that pretty mechanical toy, which, come to think of it, is what Lord Kitchener, the old field marshal, dubbed the Simms car.

So it was not only the Man Who Killed the Idea of Tanks in England who killed the idea of tanks in England!

The Man Who Killed the Idea of Tanks in England could remember when men cut grass with curved blades on the ends of sticks. What were they called again? What were those blades that seemed to whirl on the ends of sticks called? Now came Peasley riding high up on his little mower like a modish tank general, some arrogant Total War twit.

Confound him.

The Man Who Killed the Idea of Tanks in England let his dear dead wife's shawl slip from his lap. He hobbled out to the garden gate. Peasley chugged by on his mower, waved.

"Won't do!" called the Man Who Killed the Idea of Tanks in England. "Won't do at all!"

He noticed that Peasley wore some odd plastic muffs on his ears and probably had not heard him.

"Hello there!" he called, moving past the gate and onto the lawn. Peasley rounded a tree, headed straightaway at the Man Who Killed the Idea of Tanks in England. Could Peasley be driving with his eyes shut? The idiot looked lost in reverie. The Man Who Killed the Idea of Tanks in England stood motionless. His old bones, his rotted legs felt staked to the earth. What he would not give now for Hal, his old Boer War mount. Not a kingdom, though. Too late for that.

"Peasley! Peasley!"

One could not say his life flashed before his eyes. His life had been too long. The lawn mower was too slow, and clunky. He saw things, though, toys from his boyhood, tin lancers and hussars and cuirassiers, the gilt-edged pages of his beloved adventure books. He saw the nibs of examination pens, and the body of the girl who would become the woman who would become his wife, in moonlight. He saw himself and others in uniform, on parade, on maneuvers, and later on pallets, gurneys. He saw veldtgrass and Sudanese dirt and trench mud drying on his boots. He saw his mother in her maid's kit, and his father, far off in a sun-buzzed meadow, a quail gun in the crook of his arm. He saw the garish pink-and-green sleeve of *Never Mind the Bollocks*, his own palsied hand pawing at the precious vinyl inside.

It had been too bloody long, this life, everything hinging on one decision made when he was just a youngish fool with too many ribbons, too much fringe.

PEASLEY

"Won't do," said the Man Who Killed the Idea of Tanks in England, and fell to his ruined knees. Peasley, eyes shut, recollecting a childhood fishing trip he had taken with his maternal grandfather, a German who had helped develop mustard gas for the kaiser, drove down upon the Man Who Killed the Idea of Tanks in England, the blades beneath the mower's carriage whirling like, that's it, scythes.

NATE'S
PAIN IS
NOW

Nobody wanted my woe. Nobody craved my disease. The smack, the crack, the punch-outs and lockdowns, all those gun-to-my-temple whimpers about my dead mother and scabby cat—nobody cared anymore. The world had worthier victims. Slavers pimped out war orphans in hovels hung with rat-chewed velveteen. Babies starved on the desert floor.

Once, my gigs at the big-box bookshops teemed with the angry and ex-decadent, the loading-bay anarchists and hackers on parole, the meth mules, psych majors.

Goth girls, coke ghosted, rehabbed at twelve and stripping sober, begged for my sagas of degradation, epiphany. They pressed in with their inks, their dyes, their labial metals and scarified montes, cheered their favorite passages, the famous ones, where I ate some sadistic dealer's turd on a Portuguese sweet roll for the promise of a bindle, or broke into a funeral parlor and slit a corpse open for the formaldehyde. My fans would stomp and holler for my sorrows, my sins, sway in stony reverence as I mapped my steps back to sanity (the stint on a garbage truck, the first clean screw), or whatever semblance of sanity was possible in a world gone berserk with misery, plague, affinity marketing.

I had what some guy at a New Paltz book café called arc. You can't teach arc, he told me. Nobody's born with it, either. I stood for something. My finger lingered on the somehow still-flickering pulse.

I had a good run. *Bang the Dope Slowly* and its follow-up,

I Shoot Horse, Don't I?, sold big. I bought a loft, married Diana, the lovely Diana, who'd stood by in the darkness, my "research" years. My old man, the feckless prick, even he broke down and vowed his love. But as a lady at a coffee bar in Phoenix put it, what goes up can't stay up indefinitely because what's under it, supporting it, anyway?

There are wise women in Arizona.

It was here in New York City that I first noticed signs of my decline. Standing at the lectern under those harsh chain store kliegs, regaling the crowd with the particulars of a scam I used to run on Alzheimer's patients from a clinic near my squat, I heard a voice spear down from the balcony.

"Enough already!"

"Excuse me?" I said.

"I said enough," said the man. He leaned past the rail, a fattish fellow with lovely corn-blond hair. "So you almost died and hurt a lot of people along the way. You got your medal. Go home."

It was true about the medal. I'd recently won an award for creative nonfiction from a major credit card company.

"Maybe some others here want me to finish," I said, hearing my voice strain now against some sissified collapse.

"Freaking sheep," said the man.

"Leave him be!" called a voice. It sounded like Nate, my protégé. He'd been a homeless gay punk. Now he was my homeless gay punk protégé. Other voices rose to join him. My minions were protecting me. How humiliating. I felt like that bullied boy I'd described in *Spoon for the Misbegotten*, the one who ran home to weep and quaff his mother's cooking sherry—not that my mother ever cooked, let alone with sherry.

"Yeah, back off. He's been through a lot."

"He's fragile!"

"He's a fraud!" called the man, who I saw now wore heavy coveralls splotched darkly in places with what could have been berry juice, or blood.

"He's our friend!" somebody said.

"Thanks," I said. "But I can take care of myself."

There were murmurs now, mutters, maybe.

"We've got your back!"

"We're here for you, and we . . ." somebody trailed off.

"Don't you get it?" said the man in coveralls. "This guy betrayed his friends and family, he's contributed untold thousands to the drug economy, which has probably helped get others hooked, and now he blabs about it for cash. And don't start in about his philosophy. It's half-baked nonsense. He teaches us nothing. You really need this guy to tell you capitalism poisons our bodies and corrupts our souls? Are you that dim you can't figure it out for yourselves?"

Nobody spoke. I was sensing a strange mood in the crowd tonight, a balkiness I had never encountered. They were maybe beginning to be done with me.

"I think you're the dim one," I said.

"Weak meat," boomed my butcher.

It was a slow, luxuriant slide, like a dollop of half-fried mayonnaise slinking down the lean, freckled back of a teen. The teen's name was Freida, she'd designed one of my websites, but those ecstasies were over. Diana had departed. Nate had disappeared. Only my father's faxes sustained me:

Dear Disappointment,
    Not dead yet? Keep at it, kid. You had all those
sad suckers fooled, but not me. How long did you

*think it would last? The money, the women, the talks
at the Y? The Y is for some vigorous cardio and steam-
ing your nuts free of deadly nut toxins, not for listening to some junkie freak moan about his generation.
Don't you know there's real suffering in the world?
Slavers pimp out war orphans in hovels hung with rat-
chewed velveteen. I saw it on the news! Didn't you
learn anything when I was promoted to vice president
of sales in district seven and then got fired with everyone else the next day? When life knocks you down,
don't bother getting up. Because life will punish you
for getting up. Life will bite your eyes out.*

Call Me,
Your Progenitor

P.S. Dinner?

I'd pace my loft, smoke Egyptian cigarettes, drink vodka
cocktails, snort any pill I could crush. Such binges once primed
me for another recovery, another memoir, but I couldn't feel
the magic anymore, that rush of becoming. All was murk and
a sort of moister, muddier murk. Out my window was traffic,
suffering, euphoria, pretzel carts. Inside was the petty spiral. I
couldn't stop thinking about the fat dude, his wonderful hair.

I picked up my father's latest fax. Maybe a few hours in
the vicinity of his rot could put me back on track. Also, I could
teach him about the Internet. I caught a bus across the river.

My father was semiretired, a freelance consultant. He drove
around begging alms from men and women he'd once commanded. He got by, as many widowers do, on peanut butter
and hate.

"Any booze around here?" I said.

"Why don't you drink a pint of lye and get it over with?" my father said. "Why don't you have yourself a nice little lye-and-hantavirus smoothie? That'll fix you up good, you piece of shit."

My father flung himself across the table, flapped his hand in my face. It's true he never hit me. A father need not hit. His coughs, his smirks, are blows. Even a father's embrace confers a kind of violence. Or so I once pronounced on public radio.

"This meat loaf is terrible," I said now. "Worse than Mom used to make."

"It's supposed to be terrible," said my father. "This isn't meant to be a pleasant experience. This is an intervention."

"An intervention? Where is everybody?"

"Who everybody? It's just me. Nobody else cares whether you live or die. And I'm on the fence."

"Okay," I told him. "Intervene."

"I just did."

"You did?"

"Just then."

"Oh."

"So, what's the plan, Bigtime? I figure you're almost out of money. Welcome back. Maybe you could land some menial job, night janitor, say, but who's going to hire you, especially with your background as a self-aggrandizing scumrag."

"Bag?"

"Rag. Is how we said it."

"I've got to go," I said. "Thanks for the intervention."

"Anytime."

I rode back to the city, spotted this damaged-looking beauty a few seats away. The damage wasn't just the tortoiseshell tattooed over the entirety of her shaved skull, or the stern tortoise head glaring out from between her eyes. The damage, in fact, was everything not the tortoise, not the tattoo.

"I know who you are," she said.

"That makes one of us," I said.

"You mattered to me once."

"What happened?"

"You mattered to me less and less. Can you introduce me to Nate?"

"Forget Nate," I said. "You've had struggles, yes?"

"Yes."

"Lay them on me, sister."

The tortoise woman told me her story. She'd been a ward of the state, a runaway, a medievalist, a personal anal sex trainer, a robot rock chanteuse, a junior Olympic sprinter, the estranged wife of an ex–French legionnaire. Her story had heart havoc and threat, but no self-annihilation. She'd been stymied but always summoned the nerve to perdure. She was the opposite of me. I resented her and wanted to serve her. I wanted the world to pledge itself to her example.

"My God," I said.

"You have one?"

"Please," I said. "Let me write your story."

I pictured us together in my loft, me with spiral-bound pads and designer pencils worn to their nubs by her inspirational tale. Critics would applaud my decision to invest my talent in this inked slut's plight. My fans would swoon at the way I'd reached out to another wounded human. I'd get off drugs and drink for good, raise chickens upstate, produce some independent cinema.

"No way," she said. "You're a slimy, evil sellout hack."

"Sure, but will you consider it?"

The bus pulled into Port Authority. The tortoise woman slipped away.

.

Diana lived in a building near the river. Somebody buzzed me up. A man stood in the doorway, shirtless, bleeding, words freshly carved into his chest. PEEPS PLEEZER, the gashes read.

"Nate."

"Diana's not here," said Nate. "Do you want to come in? You look like hell."

"Hell is where I'm crashing these days, Nate. But what about you? You're the mutilated interlocutor here."

"I'm purging my defects via ritual."

"Is that why you're poking my wife?"

"I don't poke her. We've got something more evolved than that. Besides, you know I'm gay."

"You used to be homeless, too. Written any more bad versions of my books?"

"I no longer cite you as an influence."

"I can live with that."

"I'm having a hard time believing you can live with anything."

"Nate abandoned and betrayed me," I said.

"I'm right here," said Nate.

"I'm not talking to you. I'm talking to God. God is my witness. Tell Diana I forgive her."

"Tell her yourself," said Nate. "I'm reading downtown tonight."

"Where?"

"It's listed in most free weeklies. Diana will be there."

"Are you inviting me?"

"I'm sharing public information. Free weekly information."

.

I walked along the river for a while, wove through the queer skaters, the club kids, the breeding units with their remote-controlled strollers. I hated them, the gays, the straights. The races. The genders and ages. None of them loved me. I was feeling that forlorn hum. Maybe another memoir was burbling up.

Home, I called Jenkins, my agent.

"Nate stole my style," I told him. "My wife."

"Your agent, too," said Jenkins.

"I feel the forlorn hum coming on," I said. "It's going to be the best book yet. I've really suffered this time."

"It's over."

"What do you mean it's over?"

"It's Nate's time."

The bookstore was packed with Nate's people. They'd been my people once. I knew their faces, their fears. The tortoise woman was there in something skimpy, predatory. She was maybe pretending one of us was invisible.

Nate vaulted to the lectern in parachute pants, a fluorescent dickey. The crowd cheered as he picked a scab near his nipple, flicked it.

" 'I was a homeless gay punk,' " Nate began. " 'I was a self-hating sick fuck, too. I beat up gay people. I set homeless people on fire. Maybe it was because of my uncle, Pete. We lived in Levittown, and when I was nine . . .' " Nate read on. I noticed Diana leaning against the remainder table, her eyes rolled up under her Greek fisherman's cap, her hand frig-deep in her jeans. Behind her were stacks of my last book, going for a dollar a pop.

" 'Every time I looked up into the dirty night sky,' " Nate read now, " 'I thought of each star as one more glittering taunt I had to endure—' "

"This guy's got nothing!" I shouted. "This isn't suffering!"

Benches scraped the hardwood. Nate's people whispered, strained to look.

"He was a homeless gay punk!" somebody called.

"He set homeless people on fire!" I said.

"It's more complicated than that," said another. "He was a self-confessed self-hating sick fuck!"

"But gay!" somebody shouted.

"The two are not related!"

"In a sense they are, but only in a metaphorical sense!"

"He's not metaphorically gay," said a woman in the back.

"Leave Nate be," called the tortoise woman.

"He's poking my wife," I said. "And I have no idea why he qualifies as punk."

"I don't poke her," said Nate.

"He doesn't," said Diana. "I only need to hear his voice to come."

"Don't you get it?" I said. "There are babies turning tricks on velveteen!"

"Those babies are homeless punks, too!" somebody shouted. "Nate speaks for all of us!"

"Damn straight!"

"Nate's got arc!"

Now I felt them, the great arms bunching me up, the wisps of soft hair grazing my cheek. Next thing, I'm out on the sidewalk, staring up at that face, the one I'd never shaken from my dreams. He flashed an enormous steak knife.

"Why?" I said.

"Nate's pain is now," said the man in coveralls.

"But I have more I need to say."

"That couldn't possibly be true."

"Who are you to decide?"

"I'm the guy."

"What guy?"

"That guy. The guy out there. The guy with the pulse. When you put your finger on the pulse, it's my pulse. It's my heart. I'm the guy with the heart."

"What are those stains?" I said, pointed at his coveralls.

"That's the blood of my heart. And other hearts. Various hearts. Also, I had some berries for lunch."

"You should tell your story. Write a memoir. If you let me live, I'd be happy to help."

"I respect the genre too much," said the man, and took some practice swipes with his knife.

the
REAL-ASS
JUMBO

This world would end. The brink beckoned. A bright guy might as well pick a date. Gunderson had. A revolution in consciousness, the peaceful dismantling of mankind's cruel machinery was, according to Gunderson's interpretation of an interpretation of a pre-Columbian codex, a half decade away. But that was merely one unfolding. Alternate finales included fire, flooding, pox, nukes. *Homo sapiens* had a few years to choose. Was that time enough? For Gunderson it was time enough for another book, some lecture tours, a cable deal. Time enough to sample all the yearning young hippie tang in questing creation.

Maybe too much time. A guy could unravel.

Gunderson hadn't picked the date out of his favorite Alpacan hat. His zero hour was the culmination of a Mixtec prophecy. These bejeweled dudes had played their proto-basketball to the death, strolled the zocalo in the skins of foes. Probably they'd known something. Gunderson didn't know much about them, really, but who cared? That their glyphs foretold an imminent global shift was sufficient for Ramón, the shaman mentor Gunderson had been visiting these last several winters. That's all the convincing Gunderson needed. They'd suffered some false ends already, but you could always cite a misreading, push back the date.

Besides, nobody claimed the earth would crack open, just that something huge was on tap, and if we didn't evolve our asses quick, it would be bad huge. A reasonable message, if vague. Surprising how many preferred not to hear it. These were maybe the same folk who figured crop circles for teen pranks, the fools who called him fool. Look around, he said, to gatherings in the many hundreds, to patchouli kids and home chemists and mind hikers, to, in short, all the non-fools, the excellent few willing to be deranged by their knowing.

"Look around," he'd say, perched in loose lotus in a patron's sunken living room, and his followers would, as though exemplars of encroaching gnarlitude did ghoulish waltzes in the very room. "Look at the world, what's going on in the world. Oppression, repression, depression, the Middle This, the Western That, everything melting, burning, sick. It's no coincidence. It's prophecy, and prophecy is no joke, no matter what some cool shill for the corporations might tell you. Trust me, I used to be one of those shills. Until I got my head handed to me on a plate. Or, to be honest, in a bowl. A bowl full of the foulest soup you ever tasted. Vision gumbo. Best gift I ever got. Just a few years, people. We've got just a few years to find the better path. Or we are guaranteed one of the utmost, outmost shittiness."

Once, one of the girls who invariably stalked him home from these gigs, a Gospel of Thomas fan named Nellie, now his current sintern, while getting positively gnostic on his fun parts with ballerina slippers she'd happened to have in her bag, asked Gunderson if he ever looked out on the crowd, thought, "Suckers."

"Never," said Gunderson.

"Never?" Nellie asked, her silk insteps rubbing him toward some murked glimpse of the Demiurge.

"You don't get it," said Gunderson, apant. "This is no con."

It wasn't. It was real, and he had to share it with the world. He had to hit eyeballs. A heads-up for species-wide calamity deserved eyeballs. So, yes, he was a little on edge, on brink. He stood at the counter of Gray's Papaya waiting for a call from his manager, who was waiting for a call from his agent, who was waiting for a call from the TV people. He'd pitched them like some puma-headed god of pitching a few days before, laid waste to that conference room, but now there were concerns. They wanted to be certain Gunderson truly believed in his vision, that it wasn't a gag. Otherwise the Untitled Gunderson Prophecy Project might make for lousy television. But how could a rad Siddhartha who roved the earth quaffing potions in its most sacred places and boning its most radiant creatures, not to mention rallying humanity for one last stand against its own worst urges, make for lousy television?

Bastards had insulted him, and Gunderson could feel that hunched, bile-sopped troll he'd been, that devolved little prick he'd purged with iboga root and Jung, burble up. The old Gunderson, he knew, would never really go away. He'd just have to be endured, like some incorrigible junkie brother everybody in the family hopes will finally get clean, or just die already.

Even now the old Gunderson hovered close, craved, for instance, those glistening turd tubes on the Gray's grill rollers. Meanwhile the street stinker at the counter beside him—grease-stiff duster, foam-and-twine sandals—wolfed down a jumbo, gave Gunderson one of those poignantly exasperated looks certain nutjobs mastered, the one that asked, "Will the hologram ever cease transmission?" Bun crumbs tumbled from the man's mouth. Orphaned schizo cast out by the corporate state? Avatar of an ancient sage? Both? You never knew, but plenty of avatars burned out anyway.

Some got as lost as the old Gunderson.

Now the new, improved Gunderson sipped his papaya

smoothie. Fairly toxic, this stuff, too, but he gave himself a pass. During a recent DMT excursion in his ex-wife's duplex, while Nellie wept and shivered in the linen closet, the machine elves, or this one other-dimensional ambassador in particular, a squat, faintly buzzing fellow with scalloped metallic skin and emerald eyes, a gnome in gold lamé who'd become something of a guardian to Gunderson, ordered him to ease up.

"Relax," Baltran had said, slithering up from his usual sofa cushion crevasse. "You're doing great. You're on the verge of serious revelations. Highest clearance imaginable."

"Really? That's amazing. Thank you."

"Don't thank me. It's all your hard work. But really, relax. You're wound too tight. Get a massage or something. Rolfing's fun. Stay loose for the coming astonishments. Don't be a fuckrod."

He would not be a fuckrod. He would stay loose, stay on his toes, whatever Baltran and his glimmering ilk required. They looked like cartoons, sure, lacked sustained corporeality, and even had slightly squeaky voices, but they had chosen him. The message was too important to be left to anybody else, no matter how much he lectured at symposia about dialogue and communal deliverance. Also, no fuckrods could lurk in his vicinity. Maybe he should shitcan his manager. No sooner had he thought the phrase "shitcan my manager" than Jack's name blinked in his hand. Coincidence was a concept for sheep.

"What have you got?" said Gunderson, stepped out to the sidewalk.

"Everything's still in play," said Jack.

Gunderson's eyes strayed to the Gray's sign on the building's facade: WHEN YOU'RE HUNGRY, OR BROKE, OR JUST IN A HURRY. NO GIMMICKS. NO BULL.

There was always a gimmick. The gimmick here was you

ate factory-sealed pig chins and the hologram never ceased transmission.

"Everything's still in play? That's a good one for your tombstone."

"Thanks. I'll leave it to you to make arrangements with the engraver. Meantime, the series division is still meeting, but my guy there, my mole—don't you love it—says there will be an offer by the end of the day. They no longer have the afore-mentioned concerns. They believe you believe."

"Good."

"More than good."

"Do you believe I believe, Jack?"

"I believe in solid, serious offers."

"Fair enough. Because I don't care about the money."

"I know, I know. How about you take my cut and I take yours?"

"I would, my friend. The money's not for me. It's for Carlos."

"How is the boy?"

"He's beautiful. A beautiful child."

"Seen him lately?"

"Victoria nagging you again? I'm sorry about that. But you can't listen to all her crap. I see him plenty."

Now the reeker staggered out of Gray's Papaya, waved his ragged arms.

"Hold on." Gunderson dug in his coat for some loose bills. "Hey, buddy . . ."

"Keep your papes!" screamed the man. Particulate of frankfurter and a fine gin mist sprayed from his mouth. "I want your goddamn soul! Mean to munch it!"

"Pardon?" said Gunderson.

"Your soul wiener! That's the real-ass jumbo!"

Doubtless on the astral plane, or even just an outer ring

of Saturn, this man was delivering galaxy-beating sermons to sentient manifestations of light, but in this dimension, Seventy-Second and Broadway to be exact, Gunderson had to fucking go.

Maybe he wasn't such a bright guy. Victoria's divorce lawyer probably hadn't thought so when he brought Gunderson to ruin, or rather, to Queens. His studio in Sunnyside was suitable for the composition of prison manifestos, but Gunderson was long past garret-pacing histrionics. He'd already written his book. He'd been on the talk shows, the campus panels. A Rock and Roll Hall of Fame rock star kept inviting him up for a helicopter ride.

The Queens studio worked for hippie tang sessions, but it was not the apartment of a generational touchstone. Yet here he festered within the chipped stucco walls, beneath the hideous chandelier. He was lying on the futon after smoking some of the alpha weed, a gift, or tribute, from one of Nellie's rich friends, when he felt an odd prodding in his spine. He stood, peeled back the mattress.

"Baltran."

The machine elf's head poked through the cheap slats of the frame. Most of him seemed morphed with the hardwood floor.

"What the fuck, Gunderson? It smells like sad, lonely man in here."

Baltran's buzzing was fainter than usual. His scallops bore an odd magenta tint.

"I need to catch up on laundry."

"How about ass wiping?"

Things had, in fact, grown a wee degraded. That's why he still spent as much time as he could at Victoria's. Psychologists, probably, would offer negative explanations for Victoria's failure to change the locks, but Gunderson preferred to see it as evidence of her personal evolution. Guilt for the skill of her lawyer, too.

"Look, buddy," said Baltran, "we have to talk."

"The TV thing? I'm close. I think it has a real chance to be a wake-up call for—"

"It's about the prophecy."

"What about it?"

"The math needs a little tweaking."

"Same old same old."

"But now it's different."

"Meaning what? It's not a few years?"

"Not quite."

"What do you mean not quite?"

Baltran fell buzzless for a moment. This happened sometimes. Though his image remained, it was as though the essence of the elf were no longer present. He was perhaps being called away for an important matter. He'd be back. Baltran always came back. But Gunderson wanted him back right now.

"What do you mean not quite?" Gunderson said again, lunged. His hand sliced through the hovering projection of his friend.

"Fucking watch it, pal," the elf said, back again. "You know I can feel that. It hurts."

"Sorry."

"It's okay. I didn't mean to make you nervous. You've still got a few months."

"A few months?"

"That's time enough. Why don't you patch things up with Ramón?"

"I've got no problem with Ramón."

"Besides the fact that you don't talk to him."

"He doesn't talk to me."

"It's your business, I guess. But you've got to get out there and effect some goddamn evolution. Do me proud."

"How do I do that?"

But Baltran was gone again. He'd left Gunderson to worry all alone. How was Gunderson going to complete his mission with these new time constraints? He'd have to throw some money at the problem. You couldn't fix every problem by throwing money at it, but you couldn't fix anything without also throwing money at it. But where would he find the papes?

Sure, money came to you as long as you didn't covet it, but there was still the distinct possibility that the old Gunderson, that greedy moron, coveted on the down low, screwing them both. Maybe it was this vestigial Gunderson who'd cut off Ramón when the shaman started asking questions about the television deal. Probably just wanted a new roof for his hut. Well, unless Gunderson got the message out, Ramón wouldn't need a roof. Nobody would. There just wasn't time to waste working out the licensing on a prophecy.

Victoria was in Lisbon for a fado festival and Carlos was with his grandparents in Maine, so Gunderson had full run of the loft he'd traded in for penile liberation. Part of the excitement, the charge, of pending apocalypse, he understood, was knowing Victoria wouldn't get to enjoy this square footage much longer.

Maybe he wasn't such a bright guy for other reasons. The treatise one of his acolytes at Oxford had just e-mailed him was dense going, especially in Victoria's desktop's antiquated text format. Here were Isaac Luria and Madame Blavatsky, there a text block of dingbats. Gunderson had barely skimmed his philosophy books in college. "I get the idea," he would announce to his dorm suite after twenty minutes of deep study. "Pour me a drink."

"Psychonaut" was a silly word (Baltran said only chumps uttered it), and Gunderson had detested most of the heavy trippers in college. He'd taken hallucinogens just a few times, passed those occasions frying flapjacks, staring at their scorched, porous skins. The only acid eater he could ever abide was Red Ned, a scrawny old Vietnam vet who appeared at most major burner parties and who, in return for some My Lai-ish confession and recitations from *The Marx-Engels Reader*, got free shrooms and beer.

Once, at a barbecue, Ned cornered Gunderson near the keg, stuck a bottle under the younger man's nose, some filthy hooch he'd likely distilled in one of the bus station toilets.

"It's absinthe," said Ned. "The mighty wormwood. You will eat the devil's pussy and suddenly know French."

"Maybe later," said Gunderson.

"Later." Ned laughed. "Shit, kid, later? Later my platoon will be here. We'll slit you at the collarbone, pour fire ants in. Then you'll talk."

"I'm happy to talk now, Ned."

"You don't have anything to tell me yet. You haven't acquired the blind and pitiless truth. But I have a feeling about you. What do you think?"

"I just want to get laid."

"I'm good to go," said Ned, and gave Gunderson what might have been, during teethsome years, a toothsome smile. "You do tunnel rat zombie cock?"

"Got a rule against that."

"Your loss, son."

In short, until Gunderson had taken a magazine assignment, gone to Mexico to drink emetic potions with psychotropic turistas, his opinion of hallucinogens was that you had to worship jam bands, or believe the army had planted a chip in your head, to really enjoy them.

He'd flown to Oaxaca with a glib lede to that effect in his laptop. He returned a converso. The tales of Hofmann, the stern brain play of Huxley had never enticed him, but puking and shitting on a dirt floor while Ramón kicked him in the balls and, later, sobbing while his dead grandfather Gilbert hovered nearby in a beer-can cardigan and told Gunderson why he, Gunderson, had such a tough time being faithful to women (Gunderson's mother had hugged him too much, and his father was always on his high horse, and there was something about Gil's side of the family being related to Barry Goldwater)—all this, in aggregate, did the trick. Later he discovered the crotch kicks were not traditional, but Ramón's twist on the ritual. Didn't matter, Gunderson was hooked. A few more doses over the next several months and he knew his place in his family and his place in the infinite, at least provisionally.

He also had a vision of the world in a few years' time if the current course was not corrected. More precisely, it was a vision of North America, oil starved, waterlogged, millions thronged on the soggy byways, fleeing the ghost sprawls of the republic. He saw his sister gang-raped in an abandoned Target outside Indianapolis. The local warlord, nicknamed Dee-Kay-En-Wye for the runes on his tattered hoodie, cackled as he watched his clan work. They'd lived in Home Appliances their entire lives. Strangest of all, Gunderson didn't have a sister. This added urgency to his vision. It wasn't just about him, or his sister.

When he'd recovered and told the shaman what he'd seen, Ramón led him to a stone hut at the edge of the village. A satellite jutted from the woven roof. Inside was a sleeping cot, a computer, a bookshelf full of French Symbolists. The shaman, who to Gunderson resembled one of those carved-down distance runners he'd watched train near his father's house in Oregon, slid out a large cardboard box with copper hasps from beneath the cot. Inside was a crumbling facsimile of the storied codex. He showed Gunderson the jaguar, the sickle, the long, solstistic loops. He pointed to where the reeds ran out.

"I thought the Maya had the calendar," said Gunderson.

"Fuck the Maya," said Ramón.

Gunderson had never been much for the astronomy, the math. His colleagues, his rivals, could offer the proofs, the ellipticals, the galacticals. Most of them used the Maya Tzolkin, and Gunderson suspected that Ramón's insistence on this Mixtec forecast was just an intellectual property maneuver, but he didn't mind. He was trying to save the world, and that included not just the plants and the animals and the majestic rock formations but the people, those meat-world parasites who'd built pyramids and written concertos and enslaved their brothers and sisters and performed clitoridectomies and gone to the moon and gorged themselves on war and corn syrup. Gunderson was a people person. We just needed new kinds of people. We had to start making them right now.

The other thing that had to start being made right now was a serious offer from the TV people. Gunderson was back downtown at his favorite organic teahouse, e-mailing a fiery message to his network, hinting there might soon be an announcement about a new interpretation of the codex, a revised time frame for the Big Clambake. That would light up the boards. His people didn't need much prompting. Many were lonely sorts pining for genuine human connection or, short of that, a flash mob.

So if the series division kept wavering, maybe Gunderson could get some grass roots going. Grass roots. That had been a big word with his father. Still was, Gunderson guessed. He hadn't talked to the man in years. Why? Ask the Jaguar. Gunderson didn't know, except that maybe it was hard for men to talk to each other, especially fathers and sons, at least in this dimension. Jim Gunderson was handsome, brave, beloved, righteous. How did you talk to a father like that, a legendary activist, a lawyer for the downtrodden, ask him to read your magazine profile of a sitcom star, a charismatic CFO? Of course, Gunderson's hack days were behind him. Why didn't he call now? Because Jim Gunderson fought for a better tomorrow while his son, despite all his talk of collective action and personal evolution, was maybe just another doom pimp betting on no tomorrow at all? No, it was probably just the father-son stuff. The new times would not be so burdened. We'd be too busy line dancing with alien life-forms for patriarchal agon. Gunderson glanced up, tracked the dreadlocked teen behind the counter.

"Can I get more of this beetroot crush?"

"Of course," said the girl. "I'll bring some right over."

"That's not all you can bring."

"Excuse me?"

"Damn, sister. Look at you."

Gunderson had always subscribed to the practical man's theory of seduction: hit on everybody and everything, crudely, constantly. His percentages astonished even him.

"Yeah, you know something?" said the girl. "I've heard about you."

"What have you heard?"

"That you're, like, a genius. But also a total pigdog. I don't need that in my life right now."

"You don't need complete physical and spiritual liberation?"

"I need health insurance."

"That's the hologram talking," said Gunderson, handed her his card.

·

Outside, the sun was nearly licking him. It really felt like that, the sun the tongue of a loyal dog. Extraordinary. He stood on the curb with his eyes closed, face tilted up. This was life, its only conceivable acme. Little Carlos knew. Sweet Carlos, who had once stared up at some darkening clouds and shouted, "Don't rain, little sky!"

Gunderson was about to call Victoria's folks in Maine, something he would normally never consider, but here was this sudden surge of Carlosity. He had to talk to his son on the phone. But as soon as he thought the word "phone," the damn thing started to vibrate again.

"Jack," said Gunderson.

"They're pulling out for now. They want you to pitch again in a few months."

"What? Why?"

"Who knows? They say they've got too much in development, but it's anybody's guess. Quality television works in mysterious ways."

"Look, things are a little more complicated. We don't have a few months. We've got to do this thing now."

"What are you talking about?"

"The prophecy. There's been a change of date. A little timing snafu."

"I didn't know that happened with prophecies. Aren't they written in stone? Wasn't this prophecy, in fact, written in stone?"

"This isn't funny, Jack. This is real. I'll do it all myself. I'll get on my knees and beg Victoria for the cash. This has to happen right now. I'm through screwing around. I'll get grass roots going. This is not about a television show. This is about life on earth. Hell, I don't even know why I care anymore. Maybe it's better if we all go up in flames."

"Will you calm down? Let's just wait and see what the series division has to say in a few weeks and then—"

"And then you can tell those pigdogs to shove it up their—"

"Jeez, will you relax? Pigdogs?"

"Relax? Are you telling me to relax? You sound like fucking Baltran."

"Who's that?"

"Never mind."

"He's not that little jerk repping at—"

"No, Jack."

"I hope you're not talking to him."

"I've got to go."

Gunderson had an appointment with Nellie at the loft. They were supposed to go over scheduling. Whenever they went over scheduling, they tended to wind up naked on the carpet Victoria had bought in Tehran. Gunderson worried that their juices might agitate the dyes. Given all he'd already perpetrated upon her dignity, Victoria would probably have him jailed.

After the scheduling meeting he was supposed to meet the rock star for dinner and a helicopter ride. He'd get a call at the last minute regarding location. That's how rock stars handled scheduling. This one, an arena king from the 1980s who'd traded in his coke spoon for a yoga mat, had attended one of Gunderson's talks at an illegal ayahuasca retreat in Santa Fe and had stalked Gunderson ever since. People sneered at the rock star, his silly spiritual cant, his new music that was a parody of his old music. The man spewed platitudes, certainly, was a font of phoniness, but Gunderson sort of liked him. Or maybe he just liked being fawned over by a superannuated icon.

What you couldn't sneer at was the man's portfolio. He'd invested his money in silicon chips back when it counted.

His petty cash could probably feed the world. Would he spare some change to save it?

That Victoria was not in Lisbon, but back in what was now—and, truthfully, had always been—her magnificent home, seemed a vicious ripple in the continuum, something no blood-streaked, rainbow-feathered priest, tripping his balls off on some sun-cooked ziggurat, could ever have predicted. That she stood now on the potentially juice-marred Persian with Carlos in her arms, both of them bawling at a nearly naked Nellie, who had obviously let herself in with Gunderson's spare key and, in a perhaps-not-humorous-enough surrender of pretense, shucked off most of her wardrobe in anticipation of their scheduling meeting, signaled some kind of cataclysmic rupture in dark matter's latticework.

Not that Gunderson really knew what that meant.

"What the hell?" said Victoria as Gunderson came through the door. "This is where you bring your end times whores?"

"What happened to Lisbon?" said Gunderson.

"What happened to your self-respect?"

"What happened to knocking?" said Nellie.

"Knocking?" said Victoria. "It's my house! I'm supposed to know my ex-husband is meeting a naked slut in my house?"

"End times is more of a Christian thing," said Gunderson. "You know I don't subscribe to—"

"What exactly makes me a slut?" said Nellie. "Because I have sex? That's totally retrograde."

"Look at you," said Victoria. "The secretary. The home office screw. Except it's not even his home anymore. Talk about retrograde. I bet you think being practically a hooker is empowering, too. Is that what you think?"

"I think you're a shrill narcissist who couldn't keep pace with your husband's spiritual growth."

"Is that what he said while he rammed you with his world changer? Or did he just make you stick a ballet shoe up his butt?"

"Hey, kids!" said Gunderson. "How about both of you stop it. This is ridiculous."

"Damn straight," said Nellie. "I quit."

Nellie scooped up her clothes, seemed about to bolt, but then just stood there, quivering. Carlos squirmed out of Victoria's arms, ran to Gunderson, clutched his knee.

"Daddy!"

Gunderson squatted, squared the boy's shoulders. His son, he saw now, had the most chaotic green eyes he'd ever seen.

"I love you, Carlito," Gunderson said, sniffed sharp diaper stink. The boy was long past due for potty training, and Gunderson wondered if it was his fault, all that trauma he'd visited upon his son's developmental years. "I think he needs to be changed."

"Oh, yeah?" said Victoria. It was the old challenge. Gunderson knew he wasn't up to it. He wasn't squeamish, but he'd always preferred changing Carlos when it felt like something fun, a larkish deployment of diaper and wipe, best with an audience. So here was the deal. He'd never be a good man, a stand-up guy, a pillar, his father. His absence would have to be the honesty from which the boy could draw strength. Besides, Gunderson was a prophet, a prophet on the clock, a very scary fucking clock. Didn't that count for something?

"Yeah," said Gunderson, walked out.

•

High above the night city, he knew he'd done right. While the rock star worked the stick and hummed his old hit, Gunderson looked through the chopper's bubbled glass at the lit grid below. His strife seemed so squalid up here in the heavens, and gazing down on the bright, sick city stirred him. Maybe we were doomed fools on a dying fluke of a planet, but we'd had a damn good run. Mostly we'd murdered, tortured, razed, but once in a while we'd made something beautiful. We'd tried so hard to love.

"Thus spake Hallmark," came a voice through his headset. "Cut the humanist rah-rah, friend."

Gunderson was embarrassed the rock star had heard him get so sentimental, not to mention talk to himself.

"Aye-aye, Captain," said Gunderson.

"What's on your mind, lad? You seem perturbed."

"Do you really want to know what I'm thinking?" said Gunderson.

"Hell, no," said the rock star. "Just name the number."

"You've mastered telepathy."

"Something like that. Or maybe I can just tell that you need my help and I believe in your message enough to want to give it. I'll write the check. You lead us back from the abyss."

Screw Jack. Screw the deal. What had to be done would be done by the secret society, his brothers and sisters in vision, like this ludicrous geezer with the thousand-dollar T-shirt and spiked white hair.

Gunderson turned to thank him, to tell him of the long march ahead and the beautiful bond they would forge, but discovered the rock star slumped in his straps, stick hand listing. It was difficult to tell exactly when the spin had started or how fast the buildings roared up. The rock star was definitely dead. Maybe it was all the cocaine he'd been sneaking off to snort during dinner. Maybe it was everything he'd sniffed and jabbed and swallowed for the last forty years. Rock stars made millions singing about their broken hearts, and then their hearts actually exploded. This guy was going blue in his helmet. And he was not being a very good pilot.

Gunderson shut his eyes, saw the strewn green of his son's. He felt strange pressures on his body, was a boy again himself, waking slowly between his mother and father on their flannel sheets in Eugene, a happy little boat bumping up on warm, sloped isles. Pleasant, primal enough, this memory, suitable for the closing clip, though didn't Gunderson rate revelation, every artifice fallen away, the cosmos unmasked and Gunderson receiving the supreme briefing via transcendental brain beam? He deserved that much, didn't he? Apparently not, for here rushed the rooftops with their colossal vents, their transnational signage, penthouses lush with light and hanging gardens. Gunderson grew dizzy in his bubbled tomb. Death's smash and grab was upon him, he could feel a hand grip his arm, though it didn't seem to be the Reaper's.

"Sorry about this. Not what we were expecting, is it?"

Light twirled in the gold weave of Baltran. The elf's shimmer steadied Gunderson.

"So, it's bullshit? The calendar? The prophecy? Dimensional interface? You?"

"No, it's not bullshit," said Baltran. "It can't be."

"Are you just a figment of my imagination?"

"Fuck you. Figment."

"You told me to do you proud."

"You did do me proud, kid. I saw what you accomplished. It won't be forgotten. Not by me."

"And now what?"

"I don't know, exactly. The beat goes on?"

"The beat," said Gunderson, and he felt his phone vibrate, read the backlit text: *Serious offer.*

"Hey, shouldn't I be dead yet?" said Gunderson, looking over at Baltran. "This thing's been crashing for a while."

"Not really. That's just how you're experiencing it. Okey-dokey, here it comes, baby."

"I can feel it," whispered Gunderson. "I can taste it. It's coming on sweet."

"That might be your lozenge. See, really, there is no sweetness. What comes is pitiless, blind to you."

"Aren't we all connected?"

"Yes, we are all connected," said Baltran, "but that's not really a good thing. For the record, I always liked you, Gunderson. Breathe easy."

Gunderson watched his friend's form collapse into a sprinkly nimbus.

"Connected how?" cried Gunderson. "To what?" But he knew what, had known for some time, a few thousand years at least, back before his own shaman days on the shores of Oaxaca, longer, much longer, back before his human days, his golden molting days, his wailing vapor days, back before anything you could call a day, when he was just another stray vector shooting through great jagged reefs of anti-space. He'd known, but had he believed? Had he ever believed? Did it matter? Beyond the seal of the multiverse was a wet, blazing mouth. It slavered. It meant to munch. It had journeyed through many forevers to reach what it existed to devour: the real-ass jumbo.

Gunderson began, or ceased, to dream.

ACKNOWLEDGMENTS

Thanks to the editors who first worked with me on these stories, including Willing Davidson, Deborah Treisman, Amy Grace Loyd, Jeff Johnson, Lorin Stein, Rob Spillman, Hunter Kennedy, Jason Fulford, Michelle Orange, Tom Beller, and Joanna Yas. Thanks to Eric Chinski, who helped me make a book out of them. Thanks to the late George Kimball, whose book *Four Kings: Leonard, Hagler, Hearns, Duran and the Last Great Era of Boxing* proved a valuable source in the writing of "The Worm in Philly." Thanks to Ira Silverberg and Eric Simonoff. Thanks to Ben Marcus. Thanks to the Mac-Dowell Colony, where several of these stories were begun. Thanks to Ceridwen Morris, who encouraged me to finish them.